KATHERINE GARBERA

THE TYCOON'S FIANCÉE DEAL

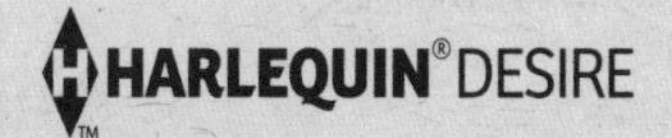

If you purchased this book without a cover you should be aware that this book is stolen property. It was reported as "unsold and destroyed" to the publisher, and neither the author nor the publisher has received any payment for this "stripped book."

Recycling programs
for this product may
not exist in your area.

ISBN-13: 978-0-373-83865-3

The Tycoon's Fiancée Deal

Copyright © 2017 by Katherine Garbera

All rights reserved. Except for use in any review, the reproduction or utilization of this work in whole or in part in any form by any electronic, mechanical or other means, now known or hereinafter invented, including xerography, photocopying and recording, or in any information storage or retrieval system, is forbidden without the written permission of the publisher, Harlequin Enterprises Limited, 225 Duncan Mill Road, Don Mills, Ontario M3B 3K9, Canada.

This is a work of fiction. Names, characters, places and incidents are either the product of the author's imagination or are used fictitiously, and any resemblance to actual persons, living or dead, business establishments, events or locales is entirely coincidental.

This edition published by arrangement with Harlequin Books S.A.

For questions and comments about the quality of this book, please contact us at CustomerService@Harlequin.com.

® and TM are trademarks of Harlequin Enterprises Limited or its corporate affiliates. Trademarks indicated with ® are registered in the United States Patent and Trademark Office, the Canadian Intellectual Property Office and in other countries.

Printed in U.S.A.

All she could think about was that big bed and Derek pleasing her.

She flushed and cleared her throat, which was suddenly very dry.

She tried to push the images out of her mind—of his naked body moving over hers. But she couldn't. She had seen him at the pool and knew his chest was solid and muscled. Now she wondered what it would feel like under her fingers.

He arched one eyebrow at her.

"What?"

"I think you just realized the most thrilling thing in this room is me."

She shook her head. "That's a lot of talk, Caruthers."

"Again with you thinking it's all ego. I promise you, it's fact," he said.

"Another promise?" she asked.

"This one I'm happy to demonstrate," he said. Derek stood up and drew her to her feet next to him. "Don't think. No more second-guessing. Let's just see where it leads."

* * *

The Tycoon's Fiancée Deal is part of the Wild Caruthers Bachelors series:

These Lone Star heartbreakers' single days are numbered...

Dear Reader,

It's the end of summer and I for one will miss the sun and long, lazy days. I'm so excited about bringing you Derek and Bianca's story. I was extremely shy in high school and there was this one guy I had a crush on. He used to talk to me at lunch, but I was... awkward and it never went any further than those few conversations before he moved on to someone not as reluctant as me.

Derek and Bianca are my way of fixing that. They were friends in high school and went on to build lives apart from each other. But the friendship stuck. Bianca is recently widowed and back in Cole's Hill, Texas, with a matchmaking mama who thinks Bianca needs a new man pronto. Except she's not ready to move on. She's not sure who she is anymore... To be honest, this heroine resonates so deeply with me.

I went through a divorce after seventeen years of marriage. It was hard to figure out what I would do next. My ideas of happily-ever-after had been shattered. I brought this to Bianca. She was married in a fairy-tale televised ceremony. In her eyes, the world expects her to still be the fairy-tale bride but life has hardened her a little. Derek's unorthodox proposal gives her a chance to reset her past and come to terms with her future.

I'm happy to tell you that, like myself, Bianca finds her faith in both herself and in happily-ever-after once again.

Happy reading,

Katherine :-)

USA TODAY bestselling author Katherine Garbera writes heartwarming and sensual novels that deal with romance, family and friendship. She's written more than seventy-five novels and is a featured speaker at events all over the world.

She lives in the UK with her husband and Godiva (a very spoiled miniature dachshund), and she's frequently visited by her college-age children, who need home-cooked meals and laundry service. Visit her online at katherinegarbera.com.

Books by Katherine Garbera

Harlequin Desire

Baby Business

His Instant Heir
Bound by a Child
For Her Son's Sake

Sons of Privilege

The Greek Tycoon's Secret Heir
The Wealthy Frenchman's Proposition
The Spanish Aristocrat's Woman
His Baby Agenda
His Seduction Game Plan

The Wild Caruthers Bachelors

Tycoon Cowboy's Baby Surprise
The Tycoon's Fiancée Deal

Visit her Author Profile page at Harlequin.com, or katherinegarbera.com, for more titles.

Sometimes we get lucky enough to meet people who will be more than acquaintances, more than friends... I've always thought of these people as kindred spirits, soul sisters. I've been very blessed to have these women in my life and on my journey, so this book is dedicated to them. Charlotte Smith, Courtney Garbera, Linda Harris, Donna Scamehorn, Eve Gaddy, Nancy Thompson, Mary Louise Wells and Tina Crosby.

One

Derek Caruthers was a badass. He knew it and so did everyone else he passed in the halls of Cole's Hill Regional Medical Center. He was one of the youngest surgeons in the country to have his stellar record and, aside from a few bumps along the way, he deserved his reputation as the best. Today he felt especially pleased with himself as he had been invited to meet with the overall hospital board. He was pretty sure he was going to be named the chief of cardiology as the hospital prepared to open its new cardiac surgery wing.

Mentally high-fiving himself, he entered the

boardroom. Most of the members were already there but the new board member wasn't. The first item of business in today's meeting was to reveal who had been chosen to oversee the new cardiac wing. Derek had no idea who it would be, but given that Cole's Hill was a small town, and he'd heard that the new board member had a local connection to Cole's Hill, Derek was confident it would be someone he knew.

"Derek, good to see you," Dr. Adam Brickell said, coming over to shake his hand. Dr. Brickell had been Derek's mentor when he first started and the two men still enjoyed a close bond. The older doctor had retired two years ago and now sat on the board at the medical center. He had been the one to put Derek's name forward for chief.

"Dr. Brickell, always a pleasure," Derek said. "I'm really looking forward to this meeting. Something I usually don't say."

"Keep that enthusiasm, but there might be a wrinkle. What if the new board member has her own ideas about the cardiology department?" Dr. Brickell said.

"Her? I've yet to meet a woman I couldn't bring around to my way of thinking," Derek said. He didn't want Dr. Brickell to see any signs of nerves or doubt in Derek. Whoever this new board member was, Derek would win them over.

Dr. Brickell laughed and clapped him on the back. “Glad to hear it.”

Derek’s phone rang and Dr. Brickell stepped away to allow him to check his call. Given that he was a surgeon he never ignored his calls.

He noticed that it was from his friend Bianca. She and he had been besties for most of their lives. It had gotten a bit awkward on his side when he’d developed the hots for her in high school but all of that had ended when she’d moved to Paris to model, fallen in love with a champion racecar driver and married him.

But for Bianca, the fairy-tale romance and marriage had been short-lived; after only three years together, her husband had been killed in a plane crash, leaving her to raise a two-year-old son alone.

Well, because of that, Derek had once again made being Bianca’s friend a top priority.

She’d been sort of fragile since she’d moved back to Cole’s Hill. He knew it was the pressure her mom was putting on her to find a husband so that Bianca and her son wouldn’t be “on their own.”

He glanced around the room and caught Dr. Brickell’s eye, gesturing that he needed to take the call. Dr. Brickell nodded and Derek stepped out into the hallway for privacy.

“Bi, what’s up?”

"I'm so glad you're here. Did I catch you before the hospital meeting?" she asked.

"Yes. What's up?" he asked again.

"Mom has another man lined up for me to go out with tonight. Is there the slightest possibility you're free?" she asked.

No, and even if he were, he wasn't going to go there. They were friends by her design and probably for his sanity, he wasn't about to rock the boat by dating her. He would cancel for her but this was Wednesday and everyone in the Five Families area where they both lived knew that the Caruthers brothers had dinner at the club and then played pool on Wednesday nights. "It's pool night with my brothers and your mom will know that."

"Damn. Okay, it was worth a shot."

"It definitely was. I'm sorry. Who is it tonight?"

"A coworker from the network. He's a producer or something," Bianca said.

Bianca's mom was a morning news anchor for their local TV station. She'd been busily setting Bianca up on dates since she'd moved back to Cole's Hill.

"Sounds…interesting," Derek said.

"As if. Mom has no idea what I want in a man," Bianca said.

And that was a can of worms Derek had no intention of opening right now. “I’ve got to go. The board is almost all here.”

“No problem. Good luck today. They’d be foolish not to pick you.”

“They would be,” Derek agreed. “Later, Bi.”

“Later.”

He disconnected the call and put his phone back in his pocket. He adjusted his tie as he looked down the hall for a mirror to check it and heard the staccato sound of high heels. He glanced over his shoulder, a smile ready, and his jaw dropped.

The woman walking toward him was Marnie Masters. Damn. She gave him a very calculated look from under her perfect eyebrows. Her blond hair was artfully styled around her somewhat angular face and teased to just the right height. She moved the way he imagined a lioness would when she sighted her prey and he didn’t kid himself that he was anything other than the prey.

“Marnie, always a pleasure to see you,” he said, though he’d been dodging her calls, texts and party invitations for the last eighteen months. So calling it a pleasure was a bit of a stretch.

“I would believe that if I didn’t have to resort to taking this role on the board and leaving my practice in Houston in order to ‘run into’ you,” she retorted.

“You’re back in Cole’s Hill?” he said, shaken. He

knew he needed to get his groove back and put on the charm.

"Well, it's the new me. Daddy donated the money for this new cardiac surgery wing—at my suggestion—and the board agreed to his suggestion that I be hired to oversee the new wing. I just finished doing something similar in Houston and Daddy really wanted me to come home… So it seems as if you and I will be working together for the foreseeable future," Marnie said.

"I'm glad to hear the board has hired someone with your qualifications," he said.

"I imagine we will get to know each other much better now that I'm working here. It will give us a chance to spend more time together and get caught up."

Derek knew he couldn't just say hell no. But there was no way he was getting involved with her again. "I'm afraid that's out of the question."

"Why? There are no rules against it," she said, with a wink. "I checked."

"Of course there aren't any rules. It's just that I'm engaged," Derek said. "I wouldn't want my fiancée to get the wrong idea."

"Engaged?" Ethan Caruthers asked as he and Derek ordered another round of drinks at the Five

Families Country Club later that night. "Why would you say something like that?"

"You know Marnie. She wasn't going to accept a no. So I panicked and..."

"Said something over-the-top. Derek, that's crazy. I think when it becomes clear you don't have a fiancée, this could backfire," his brother said.

Ethan had a point. Already, his lie had added a wrinkle to his prospects for becoming chief of cardiology. Marnie hadn't been happy to hear about the engagement and had told the board that she was considering a few other applicants. Dr. Brickell had firmly been in Derek's corner, saying that the decision needed to be made sooner rather than later, but Marnie had stood firm. She'd insisted it would be two months before the final decision would be made and had enough support from other members to win the argument and temporarily table the decision.

The board had adjourned and Derek had gone back to work, doing two surgeries that had wiped the fiancée problem from his mind until he'd shown up here. Ethan was the only one of his brothers waiting when Derek had arrived.

"Tell me about it," Derek said. "If I could just find a woman...someone who needed a guy for a few months."

"Would Marnie believe one of your casual friends was your fiancée?" Ethan asked.

"No. I told her it was someone special and that's why it was under wraps."

Ethan took another swallow of his scotch and shook his head. "Damn, boy, you always did have a gift for telling whoppers."

"I know. What am I going to do?"

"About what?" Hunter asked, joining their group. Hunter had recently moved back to Cole's Hill after spending the better part of ten years playing in the NFL and traveling the country promoting fitness while dodging the scandal of being accused of killing his college girlfriend. Recently the real murderer had been arrested and charged with the crime, which had enabled Hunter to finally break free of the dark cloud of suspicion. He was now engaged and planning the wedding of the century according to their mother and Ferrin, Hunter's fiancée. Everyone was in wedding fever in Cole's Hill.

"He needs a fiancée," Ethan said with a bit of a smirk.

Derek reached over and punched his brother. Of course Ethan would think it was funny. With only eleven months separating the two of them they were "almost twins," and as Ethan was the older of the two, he had always been a little smug.

"Do I want to know why?" Hunter asked, signaling the waitress for a drink as he sprawled back in his chair.

"Marnie Masters."

Hunter threw his head back and started laughing. "I thought you broke up with her years ago."

"It's been eighteen months," he said. He had broken up with her two years ago but had given in one night six months later when he'd been in Houston and slept with her again. It had just renewed Marnie's belief that he wasn't over her and that they should get back together. He'd been avoiding her ever since.

"So why do you need a fiancée?" Hunter asked.

"Marnie's the new board member brought in to oversee development of the surgical wing at the hospital. I panicked when I saw her and announced that I was engaged when she suggested we'd have a chance to spend time together."

"Ah," Hunter said. "Do you have someone in mind?"

"Not really," he said, but he knew that wasn't true. His mind kept pushing one face forward. She had nicely tanned olive skin, thick long black hair and the deepest, darkest brown eyes he'd ever gazed into. She was also not looking for marriage and needed a break from her matchmaking mother. He could provide her cover. But she'd have to be crazy to go along with his idea.

And she wasn't.

She was a single mom who needed her best friend to be there for her. Not come up with some scheme that would enable him to act out his long-held fantasies of calling Bianca Velasquez his.

Even if it was only for two months, three tops.

Damn.

Just then, Derek noticed her walk into the room with a guy who was a couple of years older than they were. She was smiling politely but he knew her routine. She'd brought him to the club for dinner so that when it was over she could politely bid him adieu and then walk the few blocks back to her parents' house in a nearby subdivision.

She was elegant. Graceful. The kind of woman whom dashing A-listers fell for. Not the kind of woman who'd agree to a fake engagement.

"Uh-oh," Ethan said.

"What-o?" Hunter said.

"That has never been funny," Derek said.

"It's a little funny," Ethan pointed out.

"Not tonight," Derek said.

"I'm still not caught up. Where is Nate?" Hunter asked. Nate was their eldest brother and the last of three of them to arrive. He had recently married the mother of his three-year-old daughter, Penny. Derek liked seeing his eldest brother take on the role of husband and father.

"He's running late. Something to do with taking Penny on a ride before he could drive into town," Ethan said. "Being a daddy has changed him."

"It settled him down," Hunter said. "You two should try it."

"I am, sort of," Derek said. The idea of really settling down and getting married wasn't appealing. He was married to his job. It took a lot of focus and concentration to be a top surgeon and most women—even Marnie—didn't really get that. They wanted a man who paid at least as much attention to them as the job.

"What you're doing doesn't count," Hunter said. "Bianca deserves better than a fake proposal."

"It's probably as close as I'm going to get," Derek admitted. He knew that Ethan was hung up on a woman who was married to one of his friends. So that was probably not going to happen, either. "You know we're the ones who aren't letting the gossips of Cole's Hill down. They like to think of us as the Wild Carutherses, which we can't be if we are all married up."

"I'll drink to that," Ethan said.

Derek toasted his brother and when Nate joined them a few minutes later the conversation thankfully changed from his fake engagement. Derek ate and drank with his brothers and kept one eye on the bar area where Bianca and her date were. He was ready to help her out. Like a friend would. That was all. Hunter had been right: there was no decent woman who wanted a fake fiancé.

* * *

Bianca Velasquez wasn't having the best year. She'd rung in New Year's by herself on the balcony of a royal mansion in Seville while Jose was en route to meet her. His plane had crashed and that had been… well, devastating. She'd never had the opportunity to finish her business with Jose. She'd been mad at him and had said to herself she'd hated him but the truth was he'd been her first love. They had a child together and no matter how many women he slept with while traveling the world on the F1 racing circuit, she…well, she hadn't been ready for him to leave her so abruptly.

She rubbed the back of her neck as what's-his-name droned on about a hobby he'd recently taken up. To be honest she had no idea what he was talking about. She'd zoned out a long time ago. And the thing was, he seemed like a nice man. The kind of man who deserved a woman who would engage in conversation with him instead of marking time and eating her dinner and dessert so quickly she gave herself indigestion. But Bianca couldn't be that woman.

"And I've lost you," he said.

She smiled over at him. He was good-looking and charming, everything she'd normally like in a man. "I'm sorry. This is a case of it really not being you, but me. I'm just…"

He shook his head. "I get it. Your mom mentioned

this was a long shot but I couldn't resist seeing if you were as beautiful in person as you were in your photographs."

She blushed. She'd been a full-time model by the time she was eighteen and had gotten a contract that had taken her to Paris and launched her career as a supermodel. It had been in Paris where she'd met Jose and fallen for him. But she was older now and no longer felt like that carefree girl. "Those photos were a long time ago."

"Which photos? I'm talking about the one on your mom's desk," he said.

"Oh. This is embarrassing. I am totally not my-self tonight," she said. "I'm sorry to have wasted your time."

"It wasn't a waste and if you ever feel like trying this again," he said, "give me a call."

He got up and left and she sat there at the table, staring out the windows that led to the golf course. The sun had long since set. She should head home but her son was already in bed and her mom would probably want to grill her about the date. And that wasn't going to go well.

So instead she signaled her waiter to clear away the dessert dishes and ordered herself a French mar-tini.

"Want some company?"

She glanced up to see Derek Caruthers standing

next to her table. He wore his hair short in the back and longer on top; it fell smoothly and neatly over his forehead. When they'd been kids his brownish blond hair had been unruly and wild, much like Derek himself. These days he was a surgeon renowned for his skills in the operating theater.

"I have it on good authority that I am not that charming tonight."

He pulled out the chair that her date had recently vacated and sat down. "Surely not."

"It's true. I was the most awful date. I felt like the worst sort of mean girl."

He signaled the waiter for a drink, and a moment later he had a highball glass filled with scotch and she had her martini.

"To old friends," he said.

"To old friends," she returned the toast, tapping the rim of her glass against his.

"How'd the meeting go today?" she asked. She envied Derek. He had his life together. He knew what he wanted, he always got it and unlike her he seemed happy with his single life.

"Not as I'd planned," he said.

She took a sip of her drink and then frowned over at him. "That's not like you. What happened?"

"An old frenemy showed up, making problems as is her habit and I had to shut her down," Derek said, downing his drink in one long swallow.

"How?" Bianca asked. "Tell me your troubles and I'll help you solve them."

It was nice to be discussing a problem with Derek. A problem that didn't involve her. The thirty-something who'd moved back in with her parents. She knew the gossips in Cole's Hill had a lot to say about that. From jet-setter to loser in a few short months. She pushed her martini aside realizing she was getting melancholy.

"Actually you can help me out," Derek said, leaning forward and taking one of her hands in his.

"Name it. You're one of my closest friends and you know I would do anything for you."

"I was hoping you'd say that," he said.

She smiled. Of course she'd help Derek out. He'd always been her stalwart friend. When she'd dreamed of leaving Texas and going to Paris to model, he'd listened to her dreams and helped her make a plan to achieve them. When she'd been lonely that first year, he'd emailed and texted with her every day.

"What do you need from me?"

"I need you to be my fiancée."

Two

Fiancée.

Was he out of his mind?

She shook her head and started laughing. Once she started she couldn't stop and she felt that tinge of panic rise up that she thought she'd been success-fully shoving way deep down in her gut.

"Thanks, I needed that," she said. "You have no idea what kind of week it's been."

Derek leaned back in his chair, crossing his arms over his chest, which drew the fabric of his dress shirt tight against his muscles. Distracted, she couldn't help but notice the way his biceps bulged against the fabric. One thing that had been hard for her in the years of their friendship was to ignore how hot Derek was. He worked out. He had said one time that a surgeon had to be a precise machine. And that everything—every part of his body and mind—had to be in top shape.

"I'm not joking."

"Uh, what?" she asked. She was tired. Life hadn't worked out according to her plans and if she'd thought that once she reached this age she'd have everything all figured out, she was wrong. Really wrong.

She pushed her martini glass away, feeling a bit as if she'd followed Alice down the rabbit hole. But she knew she hadn't.

"I need a fiancée," Derek said. "The new board member who holds the fate of my career in my hands? It turns out she's a borderline obsessive I dated a while ago. The only way to keep her off my back is to make sure she knows I'm off the market."

"And how do I fit into this?"

Derek tipped his head to the side and studied her. "You could use a fake fiancé as well."

She still wasn't following. She was tired and her heart hurt a little bit if she were completely honest. Derek was one of her best friends and this sounded fishy to her.

"Why?"

"So your mom will quit setting you up on blind dates. You're too kind to tell her you aren't ready to date. If we are engaged then everyone will back off and leave us alone. I can focus on wowing everyone on the board at the hospital so that they have no choice but to name me chief. You can figure out what you want to do next without the pressure your parents are putting on you."

She put her elbows on the table and leaned forward. When he put it like that she'd be a fool to refuse. "Are you sure about this?"

"I am," he said.

When wasn't Derek sure? She should have already known that would be his answer.

"If we're engaged, why would we have kept it quiet?" she asked.

He leaned in closer to her. "To give Hunter and Nate time in the spotlight. Hunter's wedding is really taking up everyone's energy."

"It is. And Kinley is busy planning it. She's going to wonder why I never even mentioned we were dating."

Bianca and Kinley were good friends. They both had been single mothers with toddlers the same age. Of course, Kinley wasn't single anymore and had found happiness with Derek's brother Nate.

Derek took her hand in his and a tingle went up her arm. "Tell her I asked you to keep it quiet."

"Hmm…it might work. Could I have until the morning to think about it?" she asked.

He nodded.

She pulled her hand away and then sat back, linking her hands together in her lap. Her palm was still tingling. She knew that saying yes would be the easy choice. But what about her son? Benito wouldn't understand that they were just pretending. Though given that he was only two years old he might not understand much of anything that was going on. He was good friends with Kinley's daughter…so he had been asking about his papa lately. He really didn't remember Jose at all.

"That sounds like it would be ideal but we live in the real world."

"Really? I hadn't realized that when I was operating on two different patients today," Derek said.

She recognized the sarcasm as one of his defense mechanisms and she didn't blame him. She was scared. The last time she trusted a man it had been Jose and his word hadn't been worth much.

"I'm not bringing this up to be difficult. I have a son. He's not going to understand why you are in our lives for a short time and then gone," she said. "We aren't twenty anymore, Derek, it's not like when you came to Monaco and we were wild. I'm a mom. You're in line to be chief of cardiology. We're…we are adults."

"Dammit. We can be adults and still be ourselves. You know me, Bi. You always have. I'm not going to disappear from your life when this is over. We're still going to be friends and I'd never cut Benito out. He's your son and just as important to me as you are."

Derek stood up. "Come on. Let's go for a walk where we can talk without worrying who might hear us."

She looked around and noticed they were gathering attention. She should have realized it sooner. "What about the pool game?"

"The boys can make do without me," Derek said. "This is more important."

There was a sincerity in his eyes; she wanted to believe in him. Well, that stunk, she thought. She'd thought she'd somehow become immune to the charm of handsome men. Of course, this was Derek and not some playboy whose parents she didn't know.

But still she'd like to think that her heart beat a little faster when he said she was important. She'd always liked Derek. He'd been one of her closest friends in middle school. He'd had the classic Caruthers good looks, but he'd been supersmart and once he'd graduated high school early and gone off to college and then medical school, they'd kept in touch first on AOL messenger, then on the different social media apps.

Years had passed before she'd seen him as an adult

and she'd been blown away by how attractive her old friend had become. Of course, she had a different life by then, but there were times when it still surprised her. She never grew tired of the strong, hard line of jaw, his piercing eyes and the way his hair curled over this forehead. There was something about him that made her want to keep looking at him.

Dangerous.

As dangerous as listening to his idea for this fake engagement. Was there ever an idea that sounded dumber?

Maybe her mom setting her up with young men she knew in the South Texas area.

"What would this entail?" she asked.

Derek didn't allow himself to relax. This was Bianca. Bianca Velasquez. She'd been the prettiest girl at the Five Families Middle School. Though he'd taken an accelerated course in Houston so he'd be able to leave Cole's Hill and go to college early, they'd always kept in touch. At first he'd thought it was because of their families. Growing up there had been a lot of cotillion dances and Junior League events where their moms had thrown them together. But then as they'd both become adults, he'd thought the crush would fade.

It hadn't.

He knew that she wasn't the girl he'd dreamed

about in middle school and high school anymore, but there was another part of him that wanted to claim her. That wanted to know that he had won over the prettiest girl from the Five Families neighborhood. That she was his.

Even just temporarily.

She was watching him cautiously. Almost as if she were afraid to trust him. That hurt.

More than it should have.

Granted, he was coming to her with a harebrained scheme, the kind that make his dad laugh his ass off at him. But she did need a break from the blind dates. And he did need a fiancée. He wasn't about to get involved with Marnie again and she would be relentless if he didn't provide a distraction.

"The hospital board has promised to make a decision in two months' time. So I'd need you to be my fiancée for about three months just so that you can attend the gala after I'm announced chief and the wing is opened," he said. Three months. That should be enough to convince him that any crush he'd had on her was well and truly dead. He could go back to being her friend and stop having hot dreams about her.

"Three months? Would we live together?" she asked. "I've been looking for a job and have some modeling gigs set up so I won't be in town continuously during that time. Would that be a problem?"

Derek leaned back in his chair trying to stay cautiously optimistic, but it seemed to him that she was almost on board with the idea. “I don’t think so. In fact, I might be able to swing some time off and go with you. It would probably enhance the entire engagement story.”

“Fair enough. What about the bachelor auction? I see you’re already on the list. Would an engaged guy be on there?” she asked.

“Yes, because we were hiding our engagement. You can bid on me and win me now,” he said with a wink.

“If we’re engaged why do I have to bid on you?” she asked with a wink back. “My brother is already into me for a month of babysitting if I win him.”

Derek had to laugh. The bachelor auction might have been one of the Five Families Women’s League’s largest fund-raisers but the men were always trying to get out of it. He just didn’t like the idea of being at the mercy of someone who’d “won” him.

“I’m offering you three months of no blind dates,” he said.

“That’s something that Diego can’t match.”

“Yeah, I’m pretty sure people would not believe you were dating your brother.”

“Thank God,” she said, laughing. This time there wasn’t the manic edge to her tone that had been there earlier when he'd first mentioned the whole engagement scheme.

"Yes. So what do you say? Are we going to do this?" he asked.

"Where would I live?" she asked.

"With me or not. Your choice," he said. "What do you want to do?"

He hadn't thought of anything beyond finding a woman who'd agree and then telling Marnie about her. But now that Bianca had mentioned living with him he knew he wanted her in his house.

Then he immediately had a vision of her in his bed. That thick ebony hair of hers spread out on his pillow, her chocolaty brown eyes looking up at him with sensual demand. Her limbs bare…

"Derek?"

"Huh?" His mind was fully engaged in the fantasy that had taken hold.

"I said, would you mind if I lived with you? I've been staying with my folks but we really need our own space."

He nodded. Living with him worked. "That sounds perfect. What do I need to do to get the place ready for you? Are we doing this?"

She leaned forward and he saw that same concern and uncertainty in her eyes and he realized that fantasies aside, he never wanted to put Bianca in a position where she was anything but a friend to him. He wanted her to be able to count on him. Even if that meant ignoring his own need for her.

"I want to say yes. Can I have the evening to think it over?" she asked, tucking a strand of her hair behind her ear. "I want to make sure I haven't missed any details and I want to run it by Benito. Make sure he's okay with another man in my life."

"He's two, right?"

"Yes, but he and I are very close and I just…after losing his father, I want to make sure he's going to be okay," Bianca said.

Derek nodded. He wasn't going to force her. He was surprised she'd considered his offer and was willing to go along with it as far as she had this evening.

"That sounds fair," he said, pulling his phone from his pocket and checking his calendar. "I don't have any surgeries scheduled for tomorrow morning so I'm free. Would you and Benito like to come over to my place for breakfast? You can check it out and he can meet me."

"Sounds like a plan."

Too bad she didn't seem so convinced of that. He wasn't too sure how to convince her. This wasn't like the operating room where he knew all the variables and could make sure nothing went wrong. This was life where he tended to make mistakes, and he really hoped this didn't turn out to be a big one.

* * *

As she sat there with Derek, Bianca knew that one night wasn't going to be enough time to ensure she made the right choice. But then a two-year-long engagement to Jose hadn't really been beneficial in hindsight. This would work. She needed it to.

She had been struggling since she'd returned to Cole's Hill. She'd stayed in Spain for nine months after Jose's death and then just after Benito had turned twenty-two months old had decided to come back to Texas but she was no closer to figuring out what was next. She was the first to admit that her knee-jerk reaction of divorcing Jose when she'd found out about his mistress had been just her way of getting out of a bad marriage. She'd never thought beyond hurting him the way he'd hurt her. Now that he was dead, she'd hoped the anger would be gone, but she knew it was still there.

And not working, living with her parents where they had a cleaning staff and wanted to hire a nanny for her, just gave her too much time to think about—dwell on—the past. It was humiliating and not productive.

This idea of Derek's was a little bit on the crazy side, she knew that, but there was a part of her that really liked it. From certain angles, she saw it as the solution to all of her problems. She wanted to be out of her parents' house and out from under their overprotectiveness. She could research some career options besides modeling and give her a chance to be the kind of mom to Beni that she wanted to be.

"Yes. That sounds good to me," Bianca repeated. She realized she might have been staring at Derek. As their eyes met something passed between them that never had before.

A zing.

An awareness.

Oh, no. Had he figured out that she'd been secretly crushing on him for the last few months? How embarrassing. She gave him her cotillion smile—the one she always used to put boys in their place back in the day—and then pushed her chair back. "I think I should be getting home."

"I'll walk you back," he said. "Or we can steal one of the golf carts."

She shook her head. "I thought we both agreed to never speak of golf carts."

"No one will suspect a thing," he said.

"That's what you thought the last time. And I'm pretty sure that the groundskeeper knew it was us, even though he could never prove it."

"I'm pretty sure you're right. So, walking might be the safer option," Derek said in that easy way of his.

She felt silly thinking that there might have been something between them. It was probably all on her side. It had been a very long time without sex—since before Beni was born—and she wasn't dead. She had been hoping she'd at least feel okay hooking up with one of her mom's blind dates. But so far it hadn't worked out.

"You okay?" he asked, coming around to hold her chair while she stood.

"Yes. Sorry. Just tired. Being 'on' with a stranger is draining," she said.

Derek put his hand on the small of her back and she felt that zing again. This time a shiver spread up her spine and she stepped aside, fumbling for her handbag.

He followed her out of the dining room. She had an account at the club like all of the families who were members, so they didn't have to settle any bill.

"I need to let my brothers know I'm leaving," Derek said.

She nodded, still more in her head thinking about what he'd asked of her. His family was large, like hers, and she understood the dynamics of having siblings around.

The evening was warm; the unseasonable heat of the day hadn't dissipated yet. The parking lot was full of cars and though it was the middle of the week it felt like the weekend. The night was busy and full of life and she realized that was what she'd been missing.

She hadn't felt busy in a long time. She wasn't saying she had the whole mothering thing licked but she and Beni had fallen into a routine where she knew what to expect. And life had become routine instead of fun. She knew that was why she was thinking of taking Derek up on this idea. It was the first unexpected thing to happen to her since…well, for a really long time.

"I'm glad you're back in Cole's Hill," he said.

"Me, too. Remember how badly we wanted to get out of here?" she asked. "I really thought modeling was going to be the life for me. I mean I figured I'd be like Kate Moss and spend the rest of my life living in the jet set…but now, I'm sort of glad that I'm right here."

"Was Benito planned?" he asked.

"That's kind of personal," she said, but only because he'd stumbled onto an argument she and Jose had had many times.

"We're going to be 'engaged' and we're friends," he said. "Just asking because your dream life didn't sound like it included motherhood."

"It didn't. With all my brothers, I never thought about having a family of my own. I figured I'd be the cool auntie to my nieces and nephews," she said.

"So what happened?" he asked.

"Well…" She paused as they turned off the sidewalk onto the path that led to the manmade lake adjacent to her parents' house. She stopped on the bridge over the lake.

"Well?"

She put one hand on the railing and looked over at Derek. He was her good friend but there were so many things about her he didn't know. The embarrassing stuff that she shared with no one. And this was something that she never needed to tell him. This bit of humiliation had died with Jose.

She looked into Derek's eyes and started to tell him what she always did when she was asked about the baby. But in her heart, she remembered Jose saying that a baby and a family would stop him from looking outside of their marriage bed for company. That a family would ground him in a way nothing else could.

Three

Derek thought she'd have some sort of easy answer. Her modeling career hadn't been conducive to children, but she came from a big family as he did. It might be a bit old-fashioned but he had assumed she would end up wanting kids after she married. But her hesitance told him there was something more to it. He'd struck a nerve that he hadn't meant to and he should have just let it go.

But this was Bianca, and there was that look of sadness in her eyes that he didn't glimpse very often. He put his hand on her shoulder, felt that spark of awareness and shoved it down. She needed a friend not a guy who was turned on by her. That damned perfume of hers wasn't helping. It was subtle and floral and when the wind blew, he couldn't help inhaling a little more deeply.

"Bia?" he asked. "It's okay if you don't want to answer me."

She just glanced over at him with those big brown eyes of hers and he was lost. He realized this was exactly how he'd let himself get friend-zoned by her. She had very emotive eyes and he had always been suckered into wanting to comfort her, to be there for. To slay dragons for her. But Jose was dead so if he was the dragon there wasn't anyone to slay.

Besides she'd had the fairy tale: first-love marriage with Jose. That wasn't the problem.

"Hey, forget I asked. I was just making small talk," Derek said even though that was the farthest thing from the truth.

He heard his old man's voice in his head: *start out as you mean to go on.* Well, lying didn't seem like a really good place to start. But he'd asked her to be his pretend fiancée, not his real one. So maybe that meant they both were entitled to their secrets.

"It's okay. It's just that once I got married my life changed… I mean my priorities changed and then I got pregnant and once I held Beni in my arms, everything just sort of…" She paused, glancing over at him and arching one eyebrow. "Don't make fun of me."

"Why would I?"

"Well, when I had my son it was like a veil was lifted from my life and I realized how shallow I had been. When I considered that little face I wanted to be more. To be better. To give him the world—not material things—but experiences. It changed me."

He could see that. She pretty much glowed whenever she talked about her son. And Derek had seen her in town with the little boy and she seemed to be in her element when she was with him. He couldn't reconcile it but she almost seemed prettier when she talked about her son.

He remembered something his brother Hunter had said once…that women in love were more beautiful. And he finally saw that. He saw it on Bianca's face when she talked about her son. He had to be very sure that he was careful when she moved in with him. She might be his secret crush from adolescence but she was a woman now, a mother, and he couldn't afford to explore a "crush" unless she was looking for the same thing.

He took a deep breath, put his hands on the wooden railing and looked out over the lake. He'd grown up on the Rockin' C but he'd spent a lot of time with his dad on the golf course and hanging out at the club after school.

And as he looked at the moonlight reflecting on the water he thought about how much his town had changed. There was now a NASA training facility on the Bar T. Bianca was a famous supermodel, his brother a former NFL wide receiver. It was crazy.

"I don't think anything has lifted a veil from my life," Derek said out loud. He was still the same inside as he'd always been: determined to do whatever he had to in order to keep on track with his medical career. He'd left the ranch at fifteen and Cole's Hill to go to college, finished undergrad in three years and then gone on to medical school. There had been no stopping him.

"Maybe that's why this setback with being named cardiology chief has been such a shock. I just have always been focused on becoming a surgeon and then on making sure I was the best."

"You are the best," Bianca said. "You're lucky, Derek. You've always known exactly what your purpose is. Some of us stumble around until we find it."

"You? You never seemed to be stumbling."

She threw her head back and laughed, and he listened to the sound of it, smiling. She had a great laugh.

"That's just because I only let people see what I want them to."

"Like the Wizard of Oz?" he asked. They'd both been in the play in middle school. He'd been the Tin Man and she'd been Dorothy.

"Just like that. 'Pay no attention to the woman behind the curtain' should be the motto for my life."

"But not now, right? You have Beni," Derek said.

She shrugged. "I'm still faking it sometimes. I mean, he has given me purpose, but being a mom is tough. Every day as I reflect on what has gone on, I wonder if I've screwed him up…that's why I want to think this engagement over. I don't want to say yes and then realize that this decision is the one that ruined him."

Derek nodded. He was pretty confident in his personal life and in the operating theater but there were times when something went wrong and he had to keep going over the surgery to see what had happened. Had he missed something? Had the error been his? How could he keep it from happening again? He'd never thought that Bianca would be like that.

She seemed confident and able to conquer anything. Seeing that she wasn't perfect made him want her even more. It made her real. Not the image of the girl he'd had a crush on, but the real woman.

This night had taken a turn and she wasn't sure she was that upset by it. She had been saying that she wanted something different to happen. That she was tired of the Wednesday night blind dates set up by her mom that coincided with her dad taking Beni and her brothers out to dinner at the Western

Two Step. Her father had missed out on bonding with Beni after his birth as they had been living in Spain. So her father was determined to make up for lost time. And the Wednesday nights with the boys were a long-established tradition in their family. It was a sports bar of sorts that had a huge gaming area in the back; they served what her father called "man food." Pretty much just burgers, steaks and fried everything. It was a tradition in their family for as long as Bianca could remember.

When she'd been in her teens every Wednesday she and her mom would have a spa night and go and get pedicures and manicures or facials or massages. And have a "girl's night out." Somehow her mom's desire to see her with a new man had taken over girl's night. Bianca knew that saying she was engaged to Derek would probably make her mom happier than just about anything else right now. The top of her bucket list was seeing her daughter happy again.

She'd said that to her.

And now she was standing next to the lake with the cicadas singing their song in the background and Derek was watching her with that too intent look of his. It was something she associated mostly with him when he was in surgeon mode. But tonight, he was concentrating on her.

She knew how important being named chief of the cardiology department was to him. He'd laid out his life plans when they were fifteen; at the time, he'd been getting ready to leave for college and she'd just gotten her first modeling job in Paris. They had been sort of thrown together as the two outsiders. The two who were leaving. And here they were again.

There was a bubble of excitement in her stomach, something that she hadn't felt since Beni had started walking and talking. She shook her head and cursed under her breath.

"What? Are you okay?" Derek asked.

She nodded wryly at him. "I just hate it when my mom is right. I mean, it would be nice if she started screwing up sometime. But every time I rail against her interfering in my life, something happens to show me she's onto something again."

"What are you talking about?" he asked.

She realized she couldn't tell him how she felt. He wanted a friend. Not a woman who was feeling all tingly and very aware of the shape of his mouth. He had a great-looking mouth. Why was she noticing it now? And now that she'd noticed it why couldn't she stop wondering how it would feel pressed against hers?

"Nothing… I think I can make it safely home from here if you want to get back to your brothers," she said. The sooner she got away from the temptation that Derek offered the better she'd be. Maybe it was just her reaction to being with a guy who—

what? The nice man her mom had set her up with had been good-looking, too. So why was she attracted to Derek and not to him?

And shouldn't that be a mark in the con column for going through with the pretend engagement?

But she knew she wasn't going to say no. Not now. Not since she'd noticed his mouth and couldn't get out of her mind if he was a good kisser or not.

It was shallow, but for once the weight that had been on her since Jose's death seemed to be long gone. She didn't feel like the hot mess she'd been. She felt almost…well, almost like her old self and there was nothing that would make her walk away from this.

She'd forgotten how fun it was to not know what was coming next. How much she enjoyed the first flush of attraction. And this was safe. Right? Derek wanted a fake fiancée. She could do that. Be close to him, have her little infatuation but protect her heart. She wasn't going to fall for Derek Caruthers. The man was married to his job.

Everyone knew that.

There was no sense in pretending that he'd ever be interested in any woman for longer than a few months. It was precisely why he'd suggested a temporary pretend engagement.

"You have the funniest look on your face," he said. "I'm not going to abandon you before I see you home. My dad would whup me if word got back to him."

She smiled because she knew he meant for her to. "You can see me to the sidewalk outside the house. If you come to the door my mom is going to grill us both and we haven't made a decision yet. You promised me time to think."

As if thinking was going to do her any good now that lust had entered the picture. She closed her eyes, desperately tried to remember what fifteen-year-old Derek had looked like. Tall, gangly, still wearing braces and with a little bit of acne, but it didn't matter because as soon as she opened her eyes she found herself staring at his mouth.

Adult Derek's mouth was lush; his lips just looked kissable. She'd kissed her fair share of men and some of the kisses had been disappointing but his mouth... he looked like he wouldn't disappoint.

"Bianca, I'm trying not to notice but you are staring at my mouth," he said.

"Mmm-hmm," she said.

"It's making me stare at your mouth and that is putting some decidedly different thoughts into my head."

"Like what?" she asked, throwing caution to the winds. Maybe he'd suck at kissing and she'd be able to walk away from him.

Or maybe not.

* * *

Derek knew he was treading very close to the edge of someplace that there would be no turning back from. He might be able to make the whole platonic-friends-helping-each-other thing work if he was able to keep his mind off the curve of her hips and the way she nibbled her lower lip when she was mulling over something. But when she looked at his mouth, chewed her lower lip…it didn't take a mind reader to figure out what she was contemplating.

And for the first time since his ill-fated affair with Marnie he was on the cusp of doing something that might derail his career goals. Because he was afraid one kiss wouldn't be enough. He wasn't ready to settle down until he'd been established as head of cardiology. He wanted to keep his focus on medicine. He needed someone like Bianca because she was respectable, well-liked and not the kind of woman Marnie would ever believe he'd coerced into being his fiancée. A smart man would remember that instead of reaching out and touching a strand of Bianca's hair as it blew in the summer breeze—and possibly blow his chance of her going along with the fake engagement.

A smart man would be taking two steps away from her instead of one half step closer and letting his hand brush the side of her cheek. Her skin was soft, but really that wasn't a surprise. She looked like she'd have prefect skin. The scent of her perfume once again drifted on the breeze and he couldn't help himself when she tipped her head to the side and her eyes slowly drifted closed.

She wanted his kiss.

He wanted to kiss her.

He leaned in and felt the soft exhalation of her breath over his jaw just before he touched her lips with his. Just a quick brush. That was all he intended but her lips were soft and parted slightly under his and he found himself coming back and kissing her again. He angled his head slightly to the right and she shifted as well and the kiss deepened. His tongue slipped into her mouth. She tasted of Indian summer and promises.

He shifted his hand on her head, cupping the back of her neck as he took all that she offered in the kiss. She was like the sweetest addiction he'd ever encountered and he knew that walking away, just forgetting this, wasn't going to happen. He wanted her.

He felt the stirring in his groin and his skin felt too tight for his body. He started to draw her closer to him but stopped. He didn't want to rush any second of this. He wanted this embrace to last forever.

Because this was Bianca. The girl who'd always been too pretty, too smart and some would say too good for him. He didn't want the kiss to end and her to come to her senses.

Maybe it was the moon or the night or the warm breeze making her forget that they were friends. That she'd friend-zoned him a long time ago but he knew he wasn't going to want to let her go. Not tonight.

But he had to.

He pulled his head back, looking down at her. Her lips were parted, moist and slightly swollen from his kiss. Her eyes slowly blinked open.

"Derek…that was…"

He put his finger over her lips. He didn't want to discuss it. "Just a kiss between friends. We're doing each other a favor and tonight, seeing you here in the moonlight, I just couldn't resist."

She chewed her lower lip for a second and then nodded. "Do you think it was an aberration? That maybe it won't happen again?"

Lying to himself was one thing, but lying to her was something else. "Honestly, I think we'd be kidding ourselves—or at least I'd be kidding myself—if I said I wasn't going to be tempted to kiss you again."

"Me, too," she admitted. "I was sort of afraid that you didn't feel the same."

"That kiss was…"

"Magic," she said. "Like you intimated earlier it was probably the pale moon and the balmy night that are making us a little crazy. We're friends. We are doing each other a favor. Complicating things by kissing each other and thinking about each other in a non-friend way—"

"Non-friend way?" he interrupted. "I didn't realize friends couldn't kiss each other."

"You know what I mean," she said, crossing her arms under her breasts in a defensive pose.

"I do. But I wanted you to know that your friendship comes first. I have to admit I've thought about kissing you since you came home this summer. I hadn't realized how much you'd changed. You're prettier than I remembered, which is saying a lot, since you were so beautiful when we were teenagers."

"Thank you. That is one of the sweetest things I've ever heard. I should be getting home," she said.

He took her hand in his and led her up off the footbridge to the sidewalk in front of her house. She didn't say anything else and neither did he. He felt like there had been too much between them for this one night. He needed her.

For his career.

And he wanted her.

For himself.

And never had he been so conflicted about what he wanted.

"I guess this is good-night."

"Good night," he said. "I'll see you and Benito in the morning?"

"Yes. Probably around eight unless that's too early."

Normally eight on a day off would be too early but this was Bianca. And he had a feeling he was going to spend a restless night remembering that kiss. And trying to figure out how he was going to keep from repeating it once she moved in with him. Unless he could sleep with her and then let her walk away. But since he'd promised to stay friends with her and her son, Derek thought it would be wiser to try to keep them from becoming lovers.

And his gut seemed to say that her answer would be yes. That they were going to be living together.

He needed a plan to keep himself together when that happened.

"That's perfect," he said.

He stood there until she entered her house and then headed back to the club.

Four

Her mom was waiting for her in the formal living room when she walked in the door. Bianca took her shoes off and then walked into the room and sat down on the settee next to her mother.

"Another dud?" her mom asked.

"Si," Bianca answered her in Spanish. "But I did have something interesting happen."

"Good. Tell me all about it," she said.

"Not yet. Probably tomorrow. I'm tired and need to process it."

Her mom reached over and pushed her hair back from her forehead. "Are you okay?"

She shrugged. She'd kept the gory details of Jose's cheating from her parents but her mom had somehow figured it out. Somehow talking about it out loud had always made her feel like it would be more real. Bianca had almost been able to fool herself into believing that no one else knew if she kept it silent.

"I'm getting there," she said. And she was. "I think you might be right that dating is a good idea."

"Of course I'm right," her mother said with a smile. "Want something to drink?"

"Not tea. Maybe sparkling water with lime."

"I have to work early tomorrow," her mom said as they approached the kitchen. Their housekeeper always kept the bar cart stocked with sliced citrus, maraschino cherries and olives.

Her mom drove to Houston very early in the morning for work at the TV station. She could have requested that the family move to Houston to make her commute easier but she never had. The Velasquez family was rooted in Cole's Hill. Bianca's father's family had settled here with a land grant from the Spanish king generations ago. The fact that they now made their money from a world-class breeding and insemination program for thoroughbred horses instead of from actual ranching didn't make a difference.

"Beni will have me up very early, too. And I have an appointment in the morning."

"That little scamp does like sunrise," her mom said. "Sit down. I'll get our drinks. I gave Caz the night off. No sense having her in the house with just me."

"Makes sense. Do you and Dad think you'll downsize any time soon?" Bianca asked. She wondered how long her parents would keep the big house now that it was just the two of them. Having her and Beni here really hadn't made a difference in the huge house. Growing up with four brothers she'd never felt crowded.

"I don't know. Your poppa doesn't want to consider moving. Instead he wants to be here for our grandkids. Are you thinking of moving somewhere else?" her mom asked.

"I don't know. I am really happy being back here and am trying to find something I can do so that Beni can grow up here, too," she said.

Her mind drifted to Derek. His idea was a sort of solution. This was what she needed to mull over. Was the risk of the attraction she felt for him worth the chance she'd have to really figure out what she wanted? The fake engagement would give her space to think. She was afraid if she kept living with her parents she'd start to want what they wanted for her and Beni. Not what she wanted for herself.

Her mom talked about the housekeeper and her father's new idea to trade his pickup in for a Harley and Bianca listened with half an ear. She missed her son. It was only a little after eight o'clock but he had a late nap on Wednesdays so he could stay out until nine with his uncles and his grandfather. She wished he were home so she could stare into his little face and try to decide if going along with Derek's idea was the right thing or not.

It was hard to believe that she was considering it. Why wouldn't she agree to it?

After that kiss she had another reason to think twice about his proposition. This wasn't as straightforward as it had been when Derek had first sat down at her table in the club and made his offer.

But she didn't regret the kiss.

How could she?

"Don't you think?" her mom asked.

"What?"

"You aren't listening to a thing I've said. Are you okay, sweetie?"

She shrugged. "Yes. But I have a decision to make and I'm not sure what to do."

"Can I help?"

"No!"

"Well, I was just offering."

"Sorry, Mom, I didn't mean it like that. This is just something I need to decide for myself. And it's weighing on my mind. I didn't mean to ignore you.

What were you saying? Something about Dad and a motorcycle?"

Her mom took a sip of her sparkling water and then reached across the table, putting her hand on Bianca's and squeezing it. "When I was trying to figure out if I should give up my job and be a stay-at-home mom like everyone expected me too, I spent a lot of time mulling things over. And in the end, well, you know I chose the morning news job."

"I know. That must have been hard, Mom," Bianca said.

"It wasn't as hard as living with the decisions afterward. The first three or four months I second-guessed everything. Should I have been home when Diego fell off his skateboard and broke his arm? Was my job the reason it happened? All of these were making me crazy and I was very unhappy. But your poppa pulled me aside one night and sat me down and said no matter what decision I had made, not picking the other choice was going to haunt me. He told me to commit to the decision I had made. And enjoy my life."

Bianca hadn't thought she needed to hear anything from her mom tonight but as always, her mom had found the exact right thing to say.

"Thanks, Mom. Every time I think I'm all grown up and know what you are going to say you surprise me."

"Good. Keeps you on your toes," she said with a wink. "Want to talk or watch a reality show?"

"Reality TV, please. I need some fake drama in my life," Bianca said.

They spent the rest of the evening watching TV until her dad and Beni got back home. Beni was dozing in her dad's arms and her father carried the little boy up to his bedroom. After her parents left, Bianca changed him into his pj's and then lay down on the bed next to her son, watching him sleep.

She wanted to say yes to Derek's proposition. And if she was very careful maybe he could be the transition between this and the next phase of her life. He wanted temporary and she had the feeling temporary was all she could really handle right now.

Plus, it was Derek. He was one of the few men she could count on always having her back and usually not expecting anything in return. And he had never asked her for anything before. She was intrigued and knew that she wanted to do it.

Why was she hesitating?

The last time she'd followed her gut, it hadn't worked out so well, she admitted.

Derek had taken the long way back to the clubhouse and now was headed to the billiards room—which was just what the club called one of the fancy private rooms that had a pool table.

"What'd she say?" Nate asked as Derek walked into the room.

What had she said? He hadn't thought of anything but that kiss and how complicated she really was. So much more than he'd anticipated when he'd first thought of asking her to help him out. But he realized now that even though they were friends there was a lot about Bianca he didn't know. He was intrigued—he'd be lying if he said he wasn't. And a part of him was worried that if she said yes she'd be a constant distraction. The other part of him was concerned if she said no that he wouldn't be able to stop thinking about the kiss and he'd go after her.

And his track record with long-term wasn't the best. So that would mean losing her completely from his life when they were done with their arrangement. He wasn't sure exactly what it was he did wrong with women but generally speaking he wasn't friends with any of the women he'd slept with.

"D? Something wrong with your hearing?" Hunter asked.

Derek gave him the finger while he opened a bottle of Lone Star beer and took a deep swallow.

"She's thinking it over," Derek said, turning to face the room and his brothers. Ethan and Nate stood near the table, while Hunter was racking the balls.

"That's not really much better than a flat-out no. Are you sure about this?" Hunter asked.

Hell, yes. If he'd had any doubts they had been amplified the minute her lips had melted under his. He rubbed the back of his neck, glanced at his watch and realized only forty-five minutes had passed since he'd left her. How was he going to make it until eight the next morning when time seemed to be moving so incredibly slowly?

But telling his brother that wasn't something Derek wanted to do.

"Yes. I've never been as sure of anything other than that I am the best surgeon in the world."

Hunter clapped him on the back. "Okay. But you know we are going to tease the hell out of you about this."

"How would that be any different than what you always do?" Derek asked. "You're forgetting that you have a honeymoon and a wedding night coming up. I think you're in for your share of teasing."

"But you also have the bachelor auction," Hunter added. "You and Ethan are going to be representing the Carutherses. Don't let us down. Or are you going to use your engagement to get out of it? I wouldn't blame you one bit."

"That's a good idea. I should line someone up. We need to bring in the big bucks like we always do," Ethan said. The auction raised money for the women and children's shelter.

"We don't always beat everyone else. The Velasquez boys beat us last year. And the Callahans think they are going to have a better shot this year because of Nate and Hunter being taken," Ethan said. "Liam was bragging about it over at the Bull Pit last night."

"How'd that go for him?" Derek asked. Ethan might be a lawyer and a damned fine one but he was also a Caruthers and they were all fighters.

"He left with a black eye and I'm wishing I'd listened to Dad and learned to lead with my left."

Derek laughed. Ethan was too much. He sensed there was something going on with his brother but right now he needed to concentrate on his own problems.

"Good," Nate said. "We only were behind the Velasquez brothers last year because Hunter wasn't here. Even if he's off the market now, he's good luck. He always brings the women with deep pockets. Remember that year you had that socialite from New York bid on you?" Nate asked.

Hunter grimaced. "Yes. She was interesting, to say the least. I'm glad I'm out of the running this year."

"Don't breathe a deep sigh of relief yet. Mom is talking about having an auction next year where wives bid on husbands to raise funds for the women's shelter."

"Ugh. Let's play pool and drink so we don't have to think about this," Hunter said. "Besides, we are supposed to be making fun of Derek and his fake engagement."

"Is it on?" Nate asked. "I thought she was thinking it over."

"I wouldn't have figured Bianca would stoop so low."

"Just proves you're not as smart as you think you are, Ethan. She's considering it. We're friends, so it's not like it's that far of a stretch."

"Whatever you say," Ethan said. "Better you than me."

They played pool and ribbed each other until two in the morning. Ethan had too much to drink and decided to bunk at Nate's apartment in town. Nate dropped him off on his way home to the family ranch and Derek walked to his house on the other side of the country club from where Bianca's family lived.

He'd bought the house once he'd decided to come back to Cole's Hill and practice medicine. He could have had a bigger career in a bigger city but it wasn't about bigger for him. It was about doing what he loved and helping the people of his community.

He let himself into his house and his dog, Poncho, came running to meet him. The pug had been a gift from his parents last Christmas. The house was empty though and he thought about how nice it would be to come home and have Bianca waiting for him.

And maybe taking her to his bed and finishing what they'd started with that kiss.

Beni woke Bianca up at five with his little hand on her face and she opened her eyes and stared into his wide-eyed gaze and smiled. She hadn't meant to fall asleep in her son's room last night. "Good morning, *changuito*."

She called him her little monkey just as her father had called her when she was little. Beni had a stuffed monkey—whom he called Gaucho—they'd gotten at the Rainforest Café in London the last time they'd been in the city.

"Morning, Mama. Didya miss me?" he asked.

"I did. That's why I slept in here with you," she said, kissing the top of his head and then ruffling his hair. "Is that okay?"

He nodded. "I missed you, too."

She hugged him close for a minute and then shifted back. "This morning we are going to have breakfast with a friend."

"Yay!" Beni said, moving with lightning speed from under the covers to sit up. "Who is it? Penny?"

"Not Penny. But we are going to see her on Friday night for a movie in the square. This is a friend of Mommy's. He's..." She trailed off. How was she going to explain to her son that Derek had asked them to live with him for a little while? "He's asked us if we want to stay with him while we are waiting to live in our own place."

"What about *Abuelo* and *Abuela*?" Beni asked.

"They'd live here. It's not far from here. We are going to take the golf cart over to his house."

"What about my car? And Gaucho?"

Bianca let her gaze drift over to the motorized miniature F1 car that Moretti Motors had sent him for his last birthday. The car was an exact replica of the one that Jose used to drive for them. She ruffled her son's hair. "All of your stuff will be there, too. Even the stuff we have in storage."

"Yay!" he said, jumping to his feet and then bouncing around on his bed. It would be nice to have her own space. Her parents had had to make one of the guest rooms into a playroom/nursery for Beni. She hadn't wanted to impose on them especially since she hadn't intended to stay her that long.

Moving in with Derek would be the impetus she needed to really get moving on finding her own place. He wasn't going to want her to stay after he received his promotion. And overnight she'd realized that one kiss wasn't really that scary. She could handle the attraction she felt for him.

She'd reminded herself they were friends first. And she wasn't all that sexual. That was one of the reasons Jose had used for having a mistress. The kiss was a fluke. One that she was determined wouldn't happen again.

Beni bounced close to the edge and Bianca grabbed him around his middle, catching him midair. She turned and pulled him down on the bed next to her.

"Tickle time," she said.

He started laughing and she felt his little fingers moving over her ribs. She laughed along with him, tickling him until her heart felt too full. She hugged her son close and thought more about this move and realized that she really was going to say yes.

She couldn't stay here in her parents' house forever. Though they'd never ask her to leave outright, Bianca realized all the matchmaking might have been her mom's way of telling her it was time to start thinking about what she was going to do with the rest of her life.

Even though she and Jose had been headed for divorce when he'd died, Bianca realized that she'd never had a chance to deal with her anger toward him. They'd fought, of course, but she'd always thought she'd see him again. She'd been so mad at him for dying that she hadn't really wanted to move on. She had unfinished business and she guessed that was why she'd been hiding out.

But Derek had given her something new to focus on. So she'd do this. She'd be his fiancée for three months. And she'd keep her lust for the surgeon under wraps so that they could both get what they wanted. A promotion for Derek and some breathing room for herself.

Beni's tummy grumbled and she sat up. "Hungry?"

"Yes," he said.

"Why don't you use the potty and then meet me on the patio for breakfast," she suggested. The sun was just starting to come up.

"Can we swim after?"

"Yes," she said. "We have to be over at my friend's at eight so we have a little bit of time."

"Yay!" he said. He'd used to say *fantástico* whenever he was excited but his new friend Penny said yay. So he'd been using that a lot more. She noticed that his language was changing from mostly Spanish to English since they'd been back in Texas. Her family spoke some Spanish but mainly English at home, which was different from how it had been when Bianca and Beni had lived in Seville near Jose's family.

"I'll leave your bathing suit on the bed," she said to him in Spanish. Though it was early autumn it wasn't cold in Texas and her parents kept their pool heated.

"*Gracias*, Mama. I love you," he replied in Spanish.

She watched him run toward the bathroom and then got out of bed. She found his racing bathing suit, a tiny Speedo that he liked to wear, and his water shoes and placed them on the end of the bed after she made it. Even though her family had always had a housekeeper her mom had insisted they make their own beds.

Bianca went into her room and donned her bikini and a cover-up. She pulled her hair up into a ponytail and then headed downstairs to get breakfast together for her and Beni. Even though it wasn't even six her mom had already headed out for work and her father had left a note saying he had gone to Austin to pick up something he'd ordered.

She and Beni had a light breakfast of fruit and then swam for an hour before she took him upstairs for his bath. She realized she was nervous and excited as she blow-dried her hair and put on her makeup. She took care using all the tips and tricks she'd learned from stylists during her years as a model to ensure she looked her best.

And only then did she feel like she was ready to go and see Derek.

She knew this was a fake engagement but the rest of the world wouldn't. Or at least that was what she told herself. Deep inside she knew that she wanted Derek to want her. Not to pity her. To see her as a woman he wanted by his side, not one he needed in order to keep his she-wolf at bay.

Five

Derek had never been around kids much. He had a new niece who was Benito's age—Penny. She was Nate's daughter but Nate had only found out about her a few months ago. So Derek and the rest of the Caruthers family were just getting to know her. Penny talked a lot. And now, as the morning progressed, Derek soon realized that Benito was a bit of a chatterbox as well.

He was adorable. He spoke English with a slight accent and he was very polite. It was also clear to Derek that Benito and Bianca had a close bond. The little boy never did anything without checking with his mom first.

While Derek had been awake most of the night waiting for Bianca to come over, this morning he'd thought a lot about her marriage to Jose and how this temporary thing he'd suggested could ever only be something between friends. Everyone—and he meant everyone in the world—knew that Bianca and Jose had been a fairy-tale love match. Her marriage had even been covered by E! and *InStyle* magazine. Not that Derek watched or read either of those things but his office manager did and she'd kept him up to date on the details.

How could she ever move on from the love of her life? And if she did, Derek suspected it wouldn't be with him. He was the rebound guy. The one who would make it easy for her transition to whoever was next in her life. And that was fine with him, he thought. He wasn't looking for more than that and neither was she.

He had brought them to the courtyard of his house. Built back in the 1980s, it was a large Spanish mission-style place with a central courtyard. There were two bedrooms on the ground floor that both opened onto the courtyard; the living room, kitchen and dining room did, too. He had a pool in the backyard and a large fire pit and outdoor kitchen. But the courtyard had a big fountain in the middle that had to be turned on. Benito had brought a stuffed monkey with him and Derek led him to the small stash of boats that Penny had played with the one time that Nate had brought her to his house.

He had asked his…well, butler sounded silly and housekeeper always made everyone think of a woman. Anyway, he'd asked Cobie, the guy who took care of the house and grounds and lived in the pool house, to make sure the fountain was on this morning and that breakfast was waiting for them on the table. It was just scrambled egg whites with spinach and turkey bacon, but Derek wanted to be able to offer Bianca and her son something to eat.

"Have you had breakfast?" he asked.

"Yes, but that was hours ago and we've had a swim, so we are hungry, aren't we?" Bianca asked her son.

"Si. Muy hambriento."

Benito ate the turkey bacon and a small portion of the eggs before asking if he could get down. Derek had noticed his eyes drifting to the fountain.

"There are some boats over by the fountain if you want to play with them while your mom and I finish eating," Derek said.

"Can I?" he asked Bianca.

"*Si*, be careful."

"Yay! I will be," Benito said. "Mama, will you watch Gaucho?"

"I will."

Bianca helped her son out of his chair. They

placed the stuffed monkey in the center of the cushion on the chair and Bianca took her son over to the fountain. Derek listened as she gave the boy a few instructions, but he was distracted by watching Bianca. She was breathtakingly beautiful this morning. She wore a slim-fitting sundress, and when she knelt next to her son to talk to him, the skirt pooled around her legs. Her arms were lean and tanned. As she stood up and turned to walk back to the table, she noticed him staring at her.

He simply shrugged. She had to be used to men staring at her.

She arched one eyebrow at him but smiled.

He stood and held her chair for her so she could sit down. Once he was seated again he took a sip of his orange juice and then folded up his napkin and placed it next to his plate. He wasn't hungry and pretending he was seemed foolish to him.

"Have you made your decision?" he asked as she carefully broke a piece of the bacon in half.

She put the bacon down on the plate and then wiped her fingers on her napkin. "I have."

He waited, expecting her to expand, but she didn't reply. Instead she pushed her sunglasses up on the top of her head, glancing over at her son, who was happily splashing the boat around in the water.

"And?"

She turned back to face Derek and nodded. "I'll

do it. I think… I think we can make this work for both of us."

Something shifted deep inside his soul and he felt a surge of excitement. "Good. Very good. I will figure out how to ask you in public so we can announce it to our families. We can say the meeting at the hospital forced us to go public before Hunter's wedding."

"Okay. I don't want to leave it too long. I've already mentioned to Benito that we might come and live with you," Bianca said. "And he's a toddler so keeping secrets is pretty foreign to him."

"That works for me. How about a dinner here on Friday night? That's tomorrow so it only gives us a little time for me to plan it and see if I can get my brothers and parents here. Can your parents attend?"

Now that she'd said yes, he wanted to get things rolling and get her moved in and his ring on her finger. Then he wanted to announce their engagement at work and at the hospital.

"I will have to change our plans. We were meant to go the movie in the square on Friday night, but I think this should take precedence. My brothers might want to come," Bianca said.

"Fair enough. My dining room seats twenty. Or I could rent a room at the club," he suggested.

"That might be more public," Bianca said. "Do you need it to be public?"

Having Bianca's agreement made him want to get

everything moving. He wanted everyone in Cole's Hill to know she was his fiancée. He knew it was temporary, but that didn't mean they had to act that way in public.

And the more people who knew about the engagement the more likely Marnie would hear about them together and then he wouldn't have to do anything other than be awesome at his job.

Being in public made her uneasy when she thought about what would be her second engagement. Everything about her marriage to Jose had been fodder for the gossip websites and part of that had been her fault. Her manager had suggested that if they publicized the wedding then she might be able to transition her career from cover model into lifestyle trendsetter—writing blogs, doing videos talking about products that her followers would then buy and showing people a slice of her life. She'd gone along with it. She had thought that it would be the next logical step in her career.

And Jose had loved the spotlight so his first instinct was to say yes. And they'd done it all. Cameras had followed them around as they made selections for the wedding ceremony. Nothing had been private and a part of Bianca had always wondered if that had been the beginning of the end for her and Jose.

"I don't need it to be public. I'm happy to have

it here. In fact we could set up some tables here in the courtyard and have dinner out here," he said. His brow was furrowed and she wondered what he was thinking.

She felt that shiver of fear down the back of her spine and realized that she'd forgotten this part of relationships. Second-guessing and never really being sure she was doing the right thing. She didn't want to start this again. What had she been thinking?

Before Jose had died but after she'd made the decision to divorce him, she'd thought she'd never get involved with another man again. It had been unrealistic but she realized now why she'd made that decision. She reached for her glass of juice, missed it and spilled it on the table.

She stood up to avoid getting any on her legs and reached for her napkin to dab it.

"Sorry about that," she said.

Derek put his hand over hers and stood up as well. "It's okay. What have I done?"

"What?" she asked.

"Something I said triggered a look of panic on your face and I don't want that. Listen, we're partners in this. We're helping each other out," he said, his voice calm and assertive.

In fact, it was so reassuring that she remembered this was her friend. Derek. She didn't have to worry that he was going to fall out of love with her and start cheating on her because they weren't in love. But they were in this temporary thing together. And a man who was trying to convince the town and his ex-girlfriend and potential new boss that he was engaged wouldn't be tomcatting around.

She took a deep breath.

"Sorry. I just remembered the craziness of my last wedding and engagement and I didn't want to repeat that."

"No problem. I prefer to keep it private. That's more our style anyway."

"We have a style?" she asked, slightly amused now that her panic had subsided.

"We do. And it's kid-friendly and family-focused," he said. "I'd like to invite my best friend and my brothers and their significant others and of course my parents but otherwise that's it."

"Same. Kinley's my best friend so she's already on the invite list. We don't have to invite her twice," Bianca said, smiling. "Let me clean this up and then we can start making a list."

"A list?" he asked, reaching around her and scooping up the plates after sopping up the juice with both of their napkins. "I got the cleanup. You stay here with Benito."

"Thank you," she said, realizing how different Derek was from Jose, who never would have touched a dirty dish. To be fair to him he had employed a fairly large staff for the three of them. But still.

"No problem. It's not the 1950s. I think I can handle cleaning up. Would you be okay if I bring Cobie back to help out with the planning? He's probably going to do the bulk of getting the courtyard ready since I've got surgery tomorrow morning."

Every word out of Derek's mouth just was further confirmation of how different he was from Jose. And she felt the last of her tension melt away.

She nodded. "That would be great."

He turned toward the French doors that led back into the kitchen and she followed him, putting her hand on his shoulder to stop him. "Thank you, Derek. I hadn't realized how much baggage I was carrying around from Jose and the way things ended with him. And this… I think this fake engagement is going to be very good for me."

He tipped his head to the side and gave her one of those smiles of his that was sweet and true and reminded her of the boy he'd been before life had shaped him into the arrogant surgeon he was today. "That's exactly what I was hoping."

He continued into the house and she turned to see Benito splashing in the fountain. He was maneuvering the boat and making huge waves with his hands. She smiled and started laughing. The sun was shining, her little boy was happy and for once she didn't feel the shadow of her past, of her doubts and of her ennui, hanging over her the way it had been for too long now.

She went over to Beni, scooped him up and kissed him on the top of his head.

"Mama! I'm playing," he said, squirming to get down.

"I know, *changuito*, I just needed a hug."

He stopped squirming and wrapped his little arms around her neck and held her tightly. "It's okay. I like your hugs."

She set him down and watched him go back to his play before realizing that it had been a while since she'd seen Derek. She glanced over her shoulder and noticed he was watching her. And the look on his face made a shiver of awareness go down her spine.

Derek knew he had to keep things cool. But seeing the expression on Bianca's face at breakfast had given him the first clue that things maybe hadn't been perfect in her marriage to that F1 racecar driver. He knew it was none of his business. They had an arrangement, but this was Bianca and he had never been able to be cool around her.

Well, he'd been able to maintain appearances on the outside, of course, but inside she'd always had the ability to stir up his base instincts and make it impossible for him to think.

Again he had that fleeting thought that this might be a mistake but there was no way he wasn't going through with it. Bianca Velasquez was going to live with him. She was going to be his fiancée.

And even if that was temporary, he was okay with it.

He struggled to keep his eyes and his mind on the planning of the party where they'd announce their engagement to their friends and family. Instead all he could think of was how long her legs were and how hot that kiss had been the night before.

He wanted another kiss. In fact his libido was hinting that they should probably practice kissing again before they had to do it in front of everyone tomorrow night. It made sense. It was logical. They had to convince the people who knew them best that this was a love match and his brothers…well, they knew the truth. He had to warn them not to say anything to anyone else.

Not that they would but he wanted to chat with them before the dinner. He didn't want to have any problems on the night of the announcement.

"You have a very serious look on your face," Bianca said. "If you don't want lights strung over the garden, it's okay to say no. Remember what you said, we're partners in this."

"It wouldn't be that hard to rig it up," Cobie said, who had now joined them in the living room. "We already have the anchors from the Christmas lights in the beams. I'm not sure if I can get all the lights we'd need in town but I could drive to Houston for more if I need them."

"I think Mom has some. I'll call and ask her if I can borrow them," Derek said. "I don't mind the lights. I was thinking about something else."

"The food? I am a pretty fair cook," Bianca said.

"No. You're not cooking the food for the party," Derek said. "Cobie, call that catering company we used for Christmas and see if they can do it."

"Cobie, would you mind giving us a minute?" Bianca said.

Cobie raised both eyebrows at her and then shrugged and turned away. "Hey, little dude, want to see the pool?"

"Mama, is that okay?" Beni asked her.

"Si," she said.

Cobie held his hand out to Beni, who took it. Derek watched them both leave.

"What's up?" he asked.

"I don't mind if you prefer a caterer but I will not have you tell me what I can't do. It sends the wrong message to Beni and personally I don't like it. I'm a grown woman and I can make my own decisions," she said.

Derek hadn't meant it the way she'd obviously taken it. "Sorry. I just meant it was a special night for you and I didn't want you working to prepare food for twenty or more guests."

"Fair enough. I think it was the delivery method. Maybe next time you could phrase it less like you were trying to boss the little woman around," she said.

"I'm happy enough to do that," he said. "Sorry if it came out that way."

"No problem. And now that I know where you're coming from, I believe a caterer would be a good idea. I think Mom has one that she uses and I know the club will cater in your home," Bianca said. "Since Cobie is handling the lights and decoration, would you like me to handle the food?"

Derek hadn't thought about asking her to plan any of this. "Sure. Do you have time?"

"Well, since I didn't get the job of receptionist at your medical group…yes, I have the time," she said. She'd applied for a job at his medical practice thinking that would give her something to do. But his office manager had pointed out that Bianca didn't have any skills to be an office worker.

"You didn't want to be a receptionist. I did you a favor," he said. "And you did a favor to Jess whom we hired because she needs the job and the money. She's going to college and had been working two part-time jobs and making less than what we're paying her now."

"That makes me feel better. But I'm still not working and could use something to occupy my time."

"I thought you had a modeling gig booked," he said. They had never really discussed what she'd be doing once they were engaged.

"I do. But it's not for a couple of weeks. We probably need to sit down and compare our schedules. That gig is in Paris. Normally I stop by Seville when I'm done with my work, to visit with my…with Jose's parents before coming back to Texas. Would you like to meet them?"

No. He most definitely didn't want to meet Jose's parents. But he had a feeling that was jealousy. "That would be fine. I'll have to check my schedule and see if I'm available. I have surgeries scheduled and of course I'm on the ER rotation. Most of my time off isn't until October."

"I had no idea," she said. "I've never really paid attention to a surgeon's schedule. I'll go by myself to Paris. And I'll make it a short trip. Might be better if you didn't meet them after all."

"Why?"

"Because this is temporary," she said. "It felt a little real for a minute and I need to remember it isn't."

He didn't want to dwell on the temporary part of it or the jealousy he'd felt when she'd mentioned Jose's parents. But the truth was in three months she'd be back out of his life and he'd be right back where he was now, except he'd be chief of cardiology at Cole's Hill Regional Medical Center.

He ignored the part where she'd said it felt real. Because no matter how hollow he felt at the thought of her leaving, he knew she would leave. And that needed to stay in the front of his mind.

Six

Derek came out of emergency surgery and washed up at the sink. The day had been long. Longer than he'd anticipated. But being on call was by its very nature unpredictable and he couldn't complain since it was also invigorating. He knew better than to ever say it out loud but there was something about having a patient come in who no one had thought would make it and then saving the person.

His skills, training and natural ability made it possible. But now that he was out of surgery he was exhausted. He cleaned up and then turned to find Marnie standing in the doorway that led to the waiting area. He had to talk to the patient's family and he really didn't have the time to deal with her.

She looked thinner than when they'd been together and she'd done something different with her eyebrows that made her look like she was scowling. She seemed so…defensive, and he hadn't even said anything to her yet.

"I have to see the family," he said. "I don't have time to discuss anything with you."

"We can talk when you're done," she said. "I have all night."

"I don't," he said.

"Oh, that's right, you have to get back to your fiancée," she said. "Who is the mystery woman?"

"We're having a dinner tomorrow night to announce it to our families and then I'll be happy to share the news with you," he said, brushing past her to walk to the waiting room and the family of his patient.

"Are you sure there is one? It doesn't seem your style to keep things quiet. I figured you'd have a skywriter do your names in a heart in the sky."

He stopped walking and turned to face her. "Really? Marnie, that sounds like something you'd like. I'm not that kind of guy. Besides, my fiancée's first marriage was very public and she'd like to keep this one quiet."

"Her first marriage? Are you sure you want to take a chance on a divorcée?" Marnie asked.

He sighed heavily. "I don't have time for this. And if I did I'd have to point out that following me around while I'm trying to work isn't exactly giving me space."

She held her hands up at shoulder level. "Sorry. I'm leaving. I look forward to hearing more about your mystery woman."

Marnie turned and headed down the hallway and Derek went to talk to the family. The patient was a high school student who'd collapsed during football practice so the family was…well, it took Derek a while to explain everything to them. He stayed with them as long as they needed to talk. The mom kept hold of his hand and said thank-you so many times that Derek was starting to feel uncomfortable. Finally, his nurse came and rescued him.

"That took forever," he said to Raine as they walked away from the family.

"Sorry, the new board member stopped by and wanted some details and it took me forever to get rid of her," Raine said.

"Marnie."

"Yes. Didn't you use to date her?"

"Don't remind me. I'm going to shower and change. Is Dr. Pitman here?" Derek asked. Pitman was a partner in Derek's practice and they checked in on each other's patients when they did rounds at the hospital.

"He just arrived. He's ready to debrief with you," Raine said. "His nurse is running late. Her kid had something after school so I'm going to stay until she gets here."

"Okay. I'll see you in the office tomorrow morning," he said. "Oh, by the way, I'm engaged."

"Engaged? I thought you said one woman couldn't tame you," she said with a wink.

Raine might work for him but they'd always had a good relationship and she treated him like a kid brother. She was ten years older and Derek had relied heavily on Raine when he'd first started practicing on his own. She had experience with people, which he'd lacked. He'd been a wiz in surgery but patients and their families had complained about his bedside manner—a lot. And Raine had been the one to help him figure out how to deal with them.

"Well, one did. Don't be surprised. I wasn't shocked when you finally roped a guy into marrying you."

She punched him in the shoulder. "Show some respect. I didn't even have to hogtie him."

"I'll remind Jer of that the next time I see him," Derek said.

"You do that," she said with a cheeky grin. "Who's the lucky girl?"

"I need you to keep it quiet. We are telling our families tomorrow night," he said.

"It won't be hard. You know I don't gossip," she said.

"I know," he said. "It's Bianca."

"Velasquez. Isn't she a model?" Raine asked. "She's the one whose husband died in the plane crash, right?"

Derek realized that everyone was going to know little pieces of Bianca's story. She was a pretty big deal in Cole's Hill because of the fame she'd found as a supermodel. "Yes. We grew up together and have been friends forever."

"Congratulations, Derek. I'm happy for you," Raine said. "Can't wait to meet her."

"Thanks," he said. Just then Raine got paged and he waved her off as he headed to the locker room to shower and change. He wanted to pretend that it didn't matter to him that everyone knew Bianca had married the love of her life. And that he could never be more than the second choice.

It was fake, for God's sake. He knew that. So why did it hurt?

Why was he upset that everyone was going to assume he was a runner-up for the woman who'd had it all?

He hated losing and he hated even more when people thought he lost. And he was still fuming, even after he'd showered, put on his clothes and got in his Lamborghini, speeding out of the parking lot and out of town toward the Rockin' C.

Bianca had arranged to meet Kinley and Penny at the coffee shop in town. The beverages were really nice and the pastries and bakery items were made here in town. Once the morning commuters were all at their nine-to-five jobs it became the place for young moms and their kids to hang.

Benito and Penny were sitting together in one of the padded armchairs. Penny had gotten a new book in the cowboy picture book series she was reading and together they were making up stories that went along with the pictures in the book.

Kinley had volunteered to go and get the drinks and as soon as her friend returned with the tray of iced tea for them all—the kids' drinks in cups with lids—Bianca glanced over her shoulder to make sure no one was close by.

"Why are you acting like a spy with some top secret info to pass?" Kinley asked.

Kinley was newly married to Nate Caruthers, the father of her child. The fact that Penny was almost three years old and that Nate—Kinley's new husband and Derek's brother—had just found out about Penny a few months ago had given the couple a few bumps but they were happy together now. Bianca noticed how easily Kinley smiled these days; it was like a weight had been lifted from her.

Which of course it had been. Keeping the secret from Penny's father had been a heavy burden for her friend.

"I have something to tell you, but don't want anyone to hear. Where's Pippa?" Bianca asked. Kinley's nanny usually accompanied her and Penny when they were in town.

"She's at home," Kinley said. "She needed some time alone today and since the bride I was supposed to meet canceled I'm free all day. So I told her to take the day. What's up with you?"

Bianca nodded. Kinley was one of the most in-demand wedding planners. She planned the weddings of A-listers and royalty, and was currently planning Hunter's wedding to Ferrin. They would be getting married at the end of the month.

"Lean in," Bianca said, putting her iced tea down and leaning forward.

Kinley did as she was told. "Okay, should we whisper?"

"I'm not being silly. I'm engaged."

"You're what?" Kinley asked, loudly.

"Kin."

"Sorry, it just took me by surprise," she said, leaning back. She glanced around to see if anyone was paying attention to them and no one was. "Who is the lucky man?"

"Derek."

"What? How is that even possible?" Kinley asked. "I think I would have known you were dating."

"We kept it quiet and everyone was busy with your impromptu wedding and the planning of Hunter's big one," Bianca said. She'd been thinking about how she was going to tell her mom, and Kinley was sort of the test run. Her chance to test out the story she and Derek had come up with and to see if it was believable.

"Wow," Kinley said. "Does Nate know?"

"I'm not sure. So far, Derek and I have just kept it between ourselves," Bianca said.

"I bet he knows. Derek and he talk a lot. That rat. He should have told me," Kinley said.

"It's not his secret to tell," Bianca said.

"Fair enough. So when did it happen?" she asked. "Where's the ring?"

"Well, we are having a party for our families tomorrow night and after that I'll wear the ring in public," she said. Actually, she didn't even have a ring; she was going to need to do something about that. She made a mental note to talk to Derek about the ring thing.

"So that's what the dinner is for," Kinley said.

"There is a lot of speculation about what was going on when you invited us all. Ma Caruthers is sure that Derek put you up to the party so he can weasel out of the Women's League bachelor auction."

"I wouldn't put it past him to try something like that. But that's not why we invited everyone to dinner."

Kinley grabbed her hand and squeezed it. "I'm so happy for you, Bianca. I love the idea of being sisters with you. Now I'm not trying to be mercenary but have you thought about a wedding planner."

"You know I want you to plan the wedding," she said because she knew that Kinley would expect her to. And she realized that the lies that she'd thought she'd have to tell by pretending to be engaged were bigger than expected. Each lie was leading to another one and she was going to be buried underneath them all.

In a way it was embarrassing that she'd lied to her best friend. She knew that her reasons were good but how was she going to fake-plan a wedding that she knew she was never going to have? She hadn't even considered this.

"Great. I can't do one for a few months. I'm slammed but I will make room for you," she said.

"That's okay. We want to let Hunter get married and then Derek is up for a promotion at the hospital so he'd have to settle in to a new job before we could marry and have a honeymoon. Just know when it's time to plan it, you're the only one I want to help with it."

Kinley nodded. "Are you sure about this? I remember watching your last wedding on TV."

"Yes. I am very sure. That was all for show and I never got to pick anything I really wanted. I had to use sponsors and what looked best in photos."

"Ugh. I mean from an industry insider I totally get why they were insistent on stuff like that, but it was meant to be your special day."

In hindsight Bianca thought maybe the chaos of that first wedding was a harbinger of what her marriage had ended up becoming.

"Yes."

"Don't worry. Derek is a great guy and when you are ready to plan it, I know this wedding is going to be spectacular."

Kinley sat back and they chatted about other things, but Bianca was startled to have that out-of-control feeling again. She wondered if it was just because for once she had something going on in her life besides planning playdates for Beni or if it were something else.

Something more to do with Derek. An image of him in a tuxedo danced through her mind. She definitely wasn't going to do any pretend marriage planning because that made everything real.

Derek arrived at the Rockin' C driving through the big fence gates that he and his brothers used to climb on and ride when they swung open. The gates were always open these days since they didn't roam the cattle up this way anymore, and he sped past them.

Suddenly he realized he had no idea what he was going to say to his parents when he got out to the ranch. But as he turned his car toward the main house where Nate lived he decided to talk to his brother first.

He parked the car in the circle drive and hopped out, bounding up the stairs to the front porch in a couple of steps. He started to let himself in then remembered that Nate and Kinley were married now and they might not want him just bursting in.

He rang the doorbell and listened to it chiming through the house. A few minutes later the housekeeper answered and directed him to the study where his brother was working.

"Why'd you ring the bell?" Nate asked as Derek came into the study and closed the door behind him.

"You're married now. Figured I shouldn't just barge in."

Nate laughed. "Very true. But Kin's in town with Penny so you're safe. What's up?"

Derek opened the little fridge in the credenza at the side of the room and took out a Dr. Pepper and offered one to Nate, who nodded. After he gave his brother his drink, Derek sat down on one of the leather guest chairs that were a new addition to the study since Nate had taken over running the ranch from their dad.

"I wanted to talk to you about tomorrow night. I need you and the boys to keep quiet about the fake engagement thing. I didn't tell Bianca that you guys know and I don't think she's going to mention it to anyone else."

"Not a problem. I'll make sure Ethan and Hunter keep quiet, too."

Derek knew his brothers would be okay. He wasn't really worried about any of them spilling the secret once they knew he wanted it kept hidden. They had always been good about having each other's backs.

"What else?"

"I need a ring for Bianca. I know it's not real but no one else will know and if I were getting engaged…" He trailed off.

"You'd give her one of the family rings," he said. "Hunter didn't use one. But he wanted something new for Ferrin after his past troubles."

"I know, it made sense, but I've always thought

when I did find the right woman I'd give her Grandma Jean's ring," Derek said. He realized that part of the reason he wanted that ring now was that it was for Bianca. If he'd asked another woman, someone whom he didn't care about the way he did Bianca, he would have gone into town to the jeweler's and picked out a ring. But this was Bianca.

"It's your ring to give to whomever you want," Nate said.

"What do you think? Is it stupid to give her that ring?" Derek asked his older brother.

Nate stood up and walked around the desk, leaning back against it. "I don't think so. You're going to need one of us to go with you to the bank to get it," Nate said. "I've got a breeder coming by in an hour so I can't go today. I might be able to do it first thing tomorrow."

"I have surgery at ten so I was going to call Pittman and see if he'd come in and open early for me," Derek said.

"That'll work for me. I don't have anything tomorrow morning except Penny. I'm taking her to school but I can bring her with me to the bank if you need to be there early so you can get to the hospital."

Derek loved that his brother had a daughter and that being a father had made huge impact on Nate's life. He wondered if a real marriage would have the same effect on him. Nate wasn't really different, he just seemed…well, happier for one thing, and more mellow. He had taken the news of his daughter well and he'd changed completely the way he used to be.

They wrapped up their plans for tomorrow morning and Derek drove back to town at a more sedate pace. Thinking about Grandma Jean's ring had made him realize that even though his career had always come first, in the back of his mind there'd been the realization that one day he'd marry.

And the thought of putting that ring on Bianca's finger seemed right. Dangerous thinking, he reminded himself. He was just getting caught up in the same fever that was infecting everyone else in his family.

Hunter was getting married, Nate had settled into married life and fatherhood… Derek needed a night out with Ethan to remind himself that he was still one of the Wild Carutherses. And this thing with Bianca was temporary.

Temporary.

But it didn't feel temporary and when she called to ask if he wanted to join her and Benito on the tennis courts, he said yes. It was only a little after six in the evening.

It wasn't what he'd planned for the evening but he didn't dwell on it. He needed to be thinking like a fiancé if he had any chance of convincing the people who knew him best and the town gossips that this was real. Marnie was going to be looking for chinks in the story and only by playing it like it was real was he going to convince her and get that job he craved.

Though when he got to the tennis court thirty minutes later and saw Bianca in her cute tennis skirt with hair pulled up in a ponytail he realized he craved her even more than the job he'd been pursuing his entire life.

Seven

Bianca had been teaching Beni to play tennis, and she used the term loosely. He had a small plastic racket and he swung it in a clunky manner at the balls. Since they'd moved back to Cole's Hill, he needed something to do outside. They already swam most of the day at her parents' house, at least when it was warm enough. So she'd thought that tennis would be fun. Mostly she imagined she'd hit the ball and he'd chase it. Which he did. But he wanted to hit the ball, too.

And it wasn't her measly athletic skills Beni had inherited but Jose's abilities for sports. He was actually pretty good with the racket. She'd gotten him a child-sized one. And she was pretty confident that once he was older he'd be able to bat the ball over the net.

Inviting Derek to join them had seemed like a good idea when she'd called him but then as she'd waited for him to show up she realized she'd done it so they could talk.

After her coffee with Kinley she realized how silly she was going to look when the engagement was over. While she didn't want to change the parameters of their arrangement, she did need to make sure that neither of them ended up being alienated from their families.

"Mama, your friend," Benito said.

She glanced at the entrance to the court they were playing on and saw Derek standing there. Benito waved at him as Derek walked toward them. The club didn't have a lot members using the courts at night and Bianca and Beni were the only ones out there.

"I'm your friend, too, Benito."

"I'm Beni. What's your name?"

"Derek. I'm Penny's uncle."

"Unca Derek," Benito asked.

Bianca rubbed the back of her neck. Uncle seemed the safest name. Or maybe just Derek. Derek looked over at her and she was at a loss.

She realized there were a couple of things she was going to have to sort out that she hadn't considered.

"Let's all go sit on the bench for a few minutes," she said.

"Okay, Mama," Beni said, skipping toward the bench in the shade at the side of the court.

Derek stopped her with his hand on her wrist.

"Is Uncle Derek a good idea?" he asked.

"Well you're Penny's uncle and our families are close. It's either that or just Derek or Dr. Derek."

"Dr. Derek sounds weird. And my brothers would make fun of me if they heard it."

"Are you coming?" Beni asked. He was sitting on the bench swinging his legs.

"Yes," Bianca said. "Listen, I'm not trying to make things harder than they have to be but we need to talk about this before tomorrow night. I want to make sure that Beni knows we're moving and when I talked to Kinley today… I just told her we're engaged. I didn't want to say it was fake." She put her head in her hands. "Oh, my God. I sound pathetic. This is a mistake."

The panic she'd felt when she thought he was going to try to manipulate her like Jose always had was nothing compared to what she felt at this moment. What kind of loser needed a fake engagement to jump-start her life? It didn't matter that she knew she wasn't doing it for any bad reasons. All of the things that Derek had said made sense. And he was her good friend.

He pulled her into his arms and just hugged her. Beni ran over. She felt his little arms around her legs and never had she felt more inadequate to be a mom than she did in this moment. She shouldn't be responsible for another person when she couldn't even get her own choices right.

"Mama," Beni said.

She pulled out of Derek's arms and stooped down by her son. Derek followed suit and soon they were a little circle of three on the tennis court. Beni had his hand on her shoulder and Derek put his hand on Beni's.

"Kiddo, your mom and I are really good friends and she and I are thinking about spending more time together. You and she would live with me, if that's okay with you," Derek said.

Beni turned to face Derek, his little face scrunched up as he studied him for a long minute. Then he nodded. "Like Penny's new papa?"

"Yes, just like that. Except I wouldn't be your papa. Your papa is watching over you from heaven so I'd just be…well, a good friend, and if it's okay with your mama, I'd be your daddy down here."

"Forever?" Benito asked, looking over at her for confirmation. She wasn't sure how to answer him.

"Yes. No matter what happens. If you and your

mom move out of my house we will still always be friends and I'll always be your daddy down here."

Bianca felt her throat tighten and realized that already Derek was being more of a father to Beni than Jose had ever wanted to be. He only needed his son for photo shoots in the winner's circle. But Derek was making an offer to Beni that Bianca knew was real.

Beni turned to her and leaned in close, whispering in Bianca's ear. "I'd like that, Mama."

She nodded. She didn't feel like a loser anymore. She realized her son needed a male influence and not just his grandfathers and uncles. He needed a man who was his own, a father who was here and not in heaven.

"I'd like that, too," she whispered back to him.

"Now that we've settled that," Derek said, "tomorrow night there is going to be a party where we will talk to everyone in our families and let them know. But for tonight I believe we are supposed to be playing tennis."

"Mama's not very good."

"Well, thanks, *changuito*, who do you think taught you?" she asked, scooping him up in her arms as she stood and shifted him around to dangle upside down while she tickled his belly.

"You did," he said between squeals of laughter and she spun him around to his feet setting him down.

"That's right. But you are better than me."

"I know!"

Derek's attitude toward the promotion and the engagement changed after that moment with Beni. He'd made a commitment to the little boy and he'd honor it. Being friends with Bianca hadn't changed in the twenty years he'd known her; he didn't anticipate that ever changing. What had started as a gut reaction and, if he were being totally honest, anger at Marnie for trying to manipulate him had suddenly gotten real.

Just like the kiss.

He might need to start avoiding these two after twilight, he thought. There was a very real danger that he'd fall for them. Like, really fall for them, and this was supposed to be temporary.

His commitment to his profession was real, too. He had three things vying for his attention right now and he had always been a man of his word. That was one of the things that the Carutherses were known for. Their daddy hadn't raised his sons to be wishy-washy or to go back on their promises or shirk their commitments.

"You okay?" Bianca asked.

"Yeah. Just thinking."

"Well, stop it. You look like you are trying to obliterate the court with your stare."

"Sorry," he said with a shrug. "What do you say we stop playing and head over to the club for a cherry Coke and maybe I teach you how to play pool."

Derek knew actually learning the game wasn't something that Beni would be able to do now but his father had started doing things like playing pool and cards with them when they were toddlers and then as they had grown up it had felt natural to play.

"I know pool. Mama and I swim lots," Benito said.

"This is a different pool with balls and sticks."

He said something to Bianca in Spanish and Derek made a mental note to start listening to the Spanish language tapes when he worked out so he could talk to them both in that language.

"Okay," Benito said. "But not soda. I like juice."

"Juice it is," Derek said. "When your mom was little she only drank pineapple juice."

"That's my favorite," Benito said.

"I'm not surprised. Bia, I walked over to meet you. I don't have my car," Derek added.

"It's okay. We brought the golf cart so we can give you a lift to the club," she said.

"Can we ride in the back?" Benito asked.

Derek wasn't sure what that meant but Benito seemed pretty excited about it. When they got to the cart he realized that Beni wanted to ride in the seat that faced backward.

"Do you mind riding with him? He's too small to ride back there by himself," Bianca said. "Or you could drive..."

"You drive. I'll ride with Beni," Derek said.

His promise to the little boy had been heartfelt but maybe a little bit impulsive. He realized that he didn't know Bianca's son at all. He was going to need to rectify that and a ride on the golf cart seemed a good place to start.

So he sat next to Beni on the back seat and put his arm around him. And when Bianca started driving the vehicle that couldn't have been going more than fifteen miles per hour he realized that there should be seat belts on the golf cart and lifted Beni off the seat and onto his lap, holding him securely with one arm.

Beni put his hands on Derek's forearm and he looked down at those tiny, chubby little hands. He'd never held a child's hand before, not even Penny's. He hadn't realized how small they were. Hell, that made him sound like an idiot but he'd never realized it.

"You two okay back there?" Bianca asked, not taking her eyes off the road.

"Yes, we're good."

Benito talked to him the entire time. Some of the words were hard to understand because he shifted between English and Spanish as he spoke. But the gist of it was that he liked speed and the wind on his face. And he laughed at lot.

When Bianca stopped in the special parking lot for golf carts in front of the club Derek was disappointed. He liked listening to Benito. But this was only the beginning.

He lifted him in his arms as he stood up, placed the little boy on the sidewalk next to him and turned to face Bianca. She looked cautiously at the two of them and then he felt Benito's hand slip into his and he knew why she was nervous.

He wanted to promise her that he'd never hurt her son. That he was a man who could make the world bend to his will. It was usually the case in life and in the operating theater but when it came to this woman and her child, he knew the stakes were higher.

She'd ceased being a girl he'd had a crush on and become a real flesh-and-blood woman to him when they'd kissed. She'd moved out of the realm of fantasy and into his real world that night. And now as her tiny son held his hand, he felt something, some emotion that was foreign to him.

It was as powerful as his connection to his patients and how he felt when he couldn't save them. There was the fear, disappointment, guilt and even a little bit of anger. He couldn't name but it felt the same in the pit of his stomach. It was something he couldn't control.

But then Bianca came over and touched his shoulder and it abated a little bit. They began walking toward the club together. He didn't allow himself to think of anything except showing Benito around the facility. He had a lot of stories about Bianca that he told to entertain the little boy and when they finally made it to the billiards room, Bianca was looking at him differently.

He thought maybe she finally saw him as a man, too. Not the awkward teenager who'd been her friend so long ago. For the first time he wondered if this might be something like love. Both of his brothers had fallen hard for women and were happy now.

But Derek had always felt like the odd duck in his family. He'd left home to go to college when he was fifteen. And though he could ride, rope and do ranch chores just like his brothers, he'd always been more of a bookworm. He was different.

But with Bianca he never felt different.

He felt…well, home.

Pool. She shouldn't be surprised that Derek wanted to teach her son to play pool. She was still grappling with how easily Beni had warmed to Derek but to be honest, she'd sort of sensed lately that he was a little bit jealous of Penny and her new father. The little girl had something that Beni hadn't been able to have until Derek.

Derek had ordered them a large pitcher of pineapple juice and had a step stool brought into the room.

The pool tables at the club were all in private rooms and all themed. This one had been recently redecorated to honor the astronauts of the Cronus mission that would be blasting off to build a space station between Earth and Mars in the next year.

There was a mural of the solar system on one of the walls. Bianca noticed that the artist was clearly old school and had put Pluto into the design despite its demotion from planet status.

She could see Derek was relishing his role as tutor and when he offered to show her how to hold the pool cue, she couldn't resist pretending she needed some help. He was arrogant and his cockiness was showing through as he told Beni that someday he'd be a great player if he paid attention.

Next it was Beni's turn. Derek lifted him onto the step stool and kept one hand on the boy's back as he took the shot. The cue ball was in his hands and he rolled it slowly down the felt, stopping well before the triangle of balls that needed a break.

"Try again. This time push a little bit harder," Derek said, moving around behind Benito and putting his own hand over her son's.

Bianca couldn't resist the image of the two of them together and pulled out her phone to snap a quick picture capturing the twin looks of concentration on their faces as they both watched the cue ball. Derek counted down from three and with his help this time

Benito broke the balls. The balls rolled around the table and a solid ball fell into the corner pocket.

"I did it."

"Of course you did. You have a very good teacher," Derek said, winking over at her.

"It's amazing there is room in here for the three of us and your ego," Bianca said.

"That's not ego, that's skill," he said.

"What's next?" Benito asked.

"Because one of the balls went into the pocket, you get to go again. Try to get all of the balls off the table."

She watched her son look over the table and she realized a split second before he moved what he was going to do. But she wasn't fast enough to stop him as reached for the solid ball closest to him and nudged it with his hand toward the pocket.

Derek caught his hand. "That's the trick. But try to do it with the cue—this one. Use this ball to knock them in."

"That's hard. Could we play different?" Benito asked.

She suspected her son was getting a little tired. It had been a long day with lots of time out and about. But Derek just nodded.

"We sure can. Actually when I was little that's how my dad taught my brothers and I to play. I was just showing off for your mom."

"What's showing off?"

Bianca waited to see how Derek would explain it and she wasn't disappointed when he said, "It's something a boy does when he likes a girl and he wants her to notice him."

"That's silly," Beni said. "Mama sees you."

"That's right, I do. He meant that he thinks he's better at playing this than I am. I don't think he was very impressed with my tennis game."

"Was that it?" Beni asked, looking back over at Derek.

"Something like that," Derek said. "It's getting late. Do you have time for ice cream before you head home?" he whispered to Bianca so that Beni wouldn't overhear.

Bianca shook her head. She wasn't sure what she was expecting when she'd invited Derek to join them but she was glad she had. But it was time for them to get home. "Not tonight. Can we give you a ride home?"

"No. A gentleman always sees a lady home. So I'll ride back to your place and then walk home from there."

"Are you sure?" Bianca asked. Her parents lived in the older section of the subdivision a good mile or so from Derek's home.

"Yes," he said. "I insist. I had a long day in surgery and could use the exercise."

"What else does a gennelman do?" Beni asked.

Derek lifted Beni off the stool and onto the floor. "He opens the door for her when he's the first one there like this."

Derek showed him as Bianca picked up her cell phone and the golf cart key and walked over to the open door.

"Thank you," she said.

"You're welcome."

Benito and Derek followed her. As they walked through the club together, she was aware that some of the patrons were watching them and she knew that it wouldn't be long before the gossip got back to her mom and to Derek's mom. It was a good thing they were having the dinner tomorrow night.

When they walked through the foyer toward the outer doors, Beni dashed around in front of her and with Derek's help, opened the heavy wood door.

She smiled down at her son. *"Gracias."*

"You're welcome," the little boy said, smiling up at her.

She wanted this little family to be real. She had to remind herself that it wasn't. That Derek could only ever be their friend. She had to remember that.

But just for tonight she was going to pretend that wasn't the case. That the man riding in the back of the golf cart with her son wasn't just her pretend fiancé but her real one.

Eight

Bianca's mom stood behind her in the bathroom, looking over her shoulder. "I don't know why we all have to go to this dinner at Derek's house. His mother doesn't know, either."

Her mom had been angling for the reason and Bianca had kept her silence. Mainly because after she'd told Kinley she'd started to realize how much confusion it was going to cause their families after they broke things off. She still wasn't sure how she was going to manage that.

She knew that she was going to have to keep her side of the bargain. Derek was proving to be a bit of an enigma. She'd gotten an email from him overnight with an invitation to a benefit at the hospital. It was to support the new cardiac surgery wing and he'd asked if she thought she could find a sitter for Beni.

It was the beginning of building a life together. And her battered heart was cheered by the invite. This was what she'd always thought couple-life would be like. It was what her parents had.

Nothing could have been further from what Jose had wanted with her than this. She realized that she was spending too much time thinking when her mom cleared her throat.

"You're going to have to wait, Mom," she said. "Just like Ma Caruthers. Derek and I will let you know what's going on once we are all together."

"It's just..."

"Ma. I promise you'll be happy about it," she said. "Oh, and I'm probably not going to be able to bid on Diego at the auction so he's going to have to find some other woman who is palatable to him to do his bidding."

"Are you and Derek dating?"

Bianca just shrugged. She suspected she was taking more joy from having this secret from her mom than she should. It was just that Ms. Bossypants was usually so in the know. She had started her career as an investigative reporter before her promotion to the morning news desk and during Bianca's teenage years her mom had shown her investigative prowess many times. It felt good to know something she didn't for once.

"Fine. Keep quiet. I can wait a few more hours to find out what's going on," she said. "Your father wants to take the big Cadillac that he just picked up two days ago."

No one would ever convince her father that anything other than a Chevrolet or a Harley was worth driving. It had been a source of amusement for Bianca watching Jose try to talk her dad into driving an Italian sports car like the one from Moretti Motors that he'd gifted her dad when they'd first started dating.

She suspected the car was still in the garage under a tarp.

"Fine. That would be nice. We need to move Beni's car seat into it."

"Dad's already on that. And you can tell Diego the bad news about the auction yourself. He's spending the night over here instead of at his place in town. He said that the Caruthers boys were drinkers and he didn't want them to think he couldn't keep up."

She laughed. Her brothers and the Carutherses had always been in competition with each other. Actually it was that way with all of the town's heritage families, the ones who'd been here since the beginning and settled the town. Some of them were big ranching families, and some, like hers, were townies. But they were all constantly trying to one-up each other in a friendly sort of rivalry.

"I will talk to him. What do you think?" she asked her mom. "Do I look okay?"

"You look better than okay. Gorgeous," her mom said. Then she leaned forward in the mirror and did something that Bianca had never seen her do before. She pushed the skin on her temples back and sighed.

There were a few fine lines around her mom's eyes but she still looked younger than her age and beautiful. "Mom, what are you doing?"

"The station suggested I get Botox and…well, what do you think?" she asked, pulling the skin taut again. "I didn't think I looked that old but with HD and all I guess I look different on air."

Bianca put her arm around her mom's shoulder. Of course, her mom looked fabulous but she worked in a medium that demanded perfection. "How serious was the suggestion? I think you look great but we know that sometimes we have no choice."

"It was truly a suggestion. Howard even said that it would be preventative before these lines started to show on camera. He also suggested I try not to smile so much," her mom said.

Howard was her mom's boss, and Bianca thought he was actually trying to help her mom, with that idea of his. She knew that. She was a model; she knew her days of modeling were numbered. After Beni's birth she'd actually been offered a few plus-sized gigs even though she wasn't truly plus-sized. When image was everything, life could be brutal.

"It's up to you. Actually, I think I might have a friend in Paris who has some products you can try before Botox. Want me to contact her? She's developing a new line."

"That would be great," Elena said. "Thank you."

Bianca squeezed her mom in a hug. "We are the only two Velasquez women. We have to stick together."

"Yes, we do."

Bianca had kept her name after her marriage to Jose because she'd had a career before their marriage. Beni's last name was a compound of hers and Jose's—Ruiz-Velasquez. They had followed the traditional way of naming using the father's surname first and then the mother's.

"So since we are the only two Velasquez women don't you think it would be a good idea to give me a heads-up on what's going to be happening tonight?"

Bianca just shook her head no and led her mom out of the room. She couldn't help feeling a tingle of excitement in the pit of her stomach.

* * *

Cobie had worked hard on the courtyard all day and it looked fabulous. As Derek took one last look at it before the guests arrived, he realized he'd wanted this night to be special for Bianca. Even though she meant more to him than he was willing to admit out loud, he had told her this was pretend. But pretend didn't have to mean something that wasn't classy and elegant. He realized that he was hoping it would impress her.

She'd made a few calls and they'd ended up with the catering service from the club. Cobie had even made sure that there was a table just for kids. To be fair there were only two children attending the party, Penny and Benito, but they had their own special area. There was even a buffet table that had been set at their level and food that had been prepared especially for them that only required fingers for eating and serving.

Ethan walked out on to the courtyard and whistled between his teeth. "Very impressive, bro. One might even think—"

"Don't say it. Didn't Nate talk to you?" he asked.

"He did. I was going to say one might even think you cared for her," Ethan said.

"Of course I do. We're friends," Derek said.

Friends. Just friends.

Even though it had been two days since that

kiss. Tonight he was hoping for another one, which was probably not the smartest idea, but he'd always been known for being book-smart and not necessarily having the best instincts outside of the operating room.

Bianca was dangerous. He knew that and he liked it.

It was part of the reason why he'd fixated on her from the beginning. Once he said he was engaged, there wasn't another woman who would fit in his mind for a fiancée besides her.

Which was more telling than he wanted to admit, even to himself.

"Just friends."

"Shut up, Ethan," Derek said.

"Okay. But this place looks like something out of a dream. You did a really nice job," Ethan said at last. "I'm glad I came back from LA for this."

"You've been on the West Coast a lot lately. Everything okay?" Derek asked. His brother looked tired, Derek noticed. He reached for Ethan's wrist and then glanced at his watch. Ethan shrugged him off and Derek let him because his brother didn't seem pale. His health was fine. So something else was going on with him.

"Yeah. Just have a client who needs a lot of attention and it can't be dealt with on the phone or via email."

"Is it almost wrapped up?"

"Yeah, I think so. He's got a kid coming and he

does a very dangerous job so I'm setting up all kinds of trusts and safeguards so that if something happens to him the kid will be covered," Ethan said.

"Sounds complicated. Just like the kind of puzzle you like to solve," Derek said.

"Yeah, it is. Some days when I'm jetting back and forth to Los Angeles or New York City I can't believe this is my life," Ethan said.

Derek nodded. "You and Hunter were always determined to get out of Cole's Hill."

"Well, Hunter more than me," Ethan said. "I like being home but I need a break sometimes, too."

"I'm feeling you," Derek said. "Last night we were up at the club and it was like the fishbowl effect as everyone watched us. It's the first time I've been aware of it. I mean, sometimes there will be something at the hospital but gossip doesn't really affect my ability to get the job done."

"You've always been a sort of wunderkind and in your own world. Focused on becoming the best surgeon."

He shrugged and nodded at his brother. "That's always been the most important thing to me."

"Still?" Ethan asked. "As I look around the courtyard, it seems like someone else might be in the running for your attention."

Derek didn't want to think about it. He'd flirted with the thought before but he'd been ignoring it.

He didn't want to contemplate that Bianca and Beni might be changing his priorities. He had to be laser-focused; that was part of what made him such a good surgeon.

"Nope. This is pretend," he said with more bravado than he felt. He wasn't about to tell his brother that Bianca had always been right there on the edge of his life and now she was closer to being in it. He wasn't sure what he'd do next.

Luckily the doorbell rang and Ethan went to the bar that Cobie had set up while Derek went to greet his guests. Cobie would have done it but Derek preferred to personally welcome everyone tonight.

He opened the door and his smile froze as he met Bianca's dark chocolate eyes. She wore a slim-fitting sheath in a silvery color that enhanced her tanned arms. A slit on the side showed off the length of her leg. She had on a pair of impossibly high heels, making her almost as tall as Derek.

She had her hair pulled up in one of those fancy ways women wore their hair for events but a tendril had slipped loose and curled against her cheek. He licked his suddenly dry lips and stood there as though he'd never seen a girl before.

And maybe he hadn't. He certainly hadn't seen a woman who took his breath away like Bianca did.

"Won't you come in," he said, stepping back to allow her to enter.

* * *

Seeing everyone together tonight made Bianca realize how many men there were in their combined families. She wasn't overwhelmed but she noticed that Kinley seemed…well, out of her element. She wondered if it was simply that she was getting used to being part of this large family.

She knew how much her friend had struggled on her own after getting pregnant and giving birth to Penny. Kinley had asked if she could bring Pippa to the party and Bianca had agreed. Pippa now sat at the end of the table between Diego and Inigo. Whatever she was saying was keeping her brothers enchanted or maybe it was her British accent or the air of mystery about her.

Nate seemed to notice Kinley's unease and put his arm around her, whispering something in her ear that made her blush and then smile up at him. That was when Bianca, who'd been feeling pretty confident that she was okay with the whole fake fiancée arrangement, suddenly realized she wasn't.

Kinley had something real. Something that Bianca knew she'd always wanted. Something that everyone grew up believing they'd find as adults. Love. Didn't everyone? Didn't everyone want to be held and made to feel like they weren't alone? Bianca did.

She'd thought those dreams and desires had died with Jose but knew they hadn't.

Benito was close to what she wanted. She had poured her love into her little boy but she knew he'd grow up and someday be an adult on his own. She wanted a man to share her life with. She wasn't sure that pretending wasn't the way to get to that. But she wanted someone who was really hers.

Like that party invite that Derek had sent to her earlier. It meant blending their lives so when she attended an event she didn't have to wonder who would be there. If she'd have someone to talk to. A partner could be that. The right partner, she thought. Jose hadn't been that for her.

He definitely hadn't been that after they got married because he'd still been too busy proving he was the hottest guy on the F1 circuit. It was hard because the drivers were arrogant, spoiled and used to women falling all over them. Fair enough. There was something about all the rare masculine power that they exuded.

Derek had it, too. But her view of him was tempered by the fact that she'd known him as a boy. She saw past his arrogance and the cocky charm he wielded effortlessly. But that didn't mean he wouldn't hurt her.

He'd asked for temporary.

She had to remind herself of that fact constantly because of the way he acted at times. Last night in the club's billiards room. Tonight with his enchanting courtyard that looked like something out of a Hollywood romance movie set. Or when he glanced over at her and winked at her.

She felt something clench deep inside of her. She was falling for him. It didn't matter how many times she said "temporary" in her head.

Her heart didn't feel like this was make-believe.

Not at all.

Derek clinked his fork on the side of his wine-glass to get everyone's attention and the conversation slowly stopped.

He stood up and then looked over at her, and she felt that nervous excitement again. It felt like there were butterflies in her stomach or more as though she'd swallowed the sun. She felt hot like she was blushing.

"Thank you everyone for coming here tonight on such short notice. I realize that we've kept you in suspense about why we wanted you all here. Bianca and I have a very special announcement."

He held his hand out to her and she took it and stood up. They hadn't rehearsed this and she wasn't sure what she was supposed to say. She tried to remember all of the things that she'd said to Kinley yesterday but her mind was blank. She was simply staring into Derek's blue eyes. She saw that curl that he tried to tame that had fallen forward on his forehead. And when their eyes met her panic stilled.

This was Derek. Her friend. The one man who wasn't a blood relative whom she could count on. She'd always been able to count on him and this was no different.

He lifted her hand and kissed the back of it. And then she felt him slipping something on her finger and she glanced down to see a charming antique engagement ring with a solitaire diamond set in a platinum band.

"I've asked Bianca to marry me and she's said yes. We've been keeping it quiet recently because of Nate's marriage to Kinley and of course Hunter and Ferrin's big day. We didn't want to steal anyone's thunder. But we figured it might be okay to let our families in on the secret," Derek said.

He put his arm around Bianca as everyone clapped for them. Her parents got to their feet as did Derek's and the two of them were surrounded by their folks and their brothers. Her mom hugged her close.

"No wonder all those blind dates didn't work out. You should have mentioned you were seeing someone," her mom said.

"I always thought there was more to the two of you than just friends," Ma Caruthers said, hugging Bianca after her mom let go.

"Well, friendship is a great way to start a relationship," she said.

"Very true," her mom agreed.

"My sons have good taste in women," Mr. Caruthers said, hugging her close.

"We learned from your example, Dad," Derek said with a wink.

She noticed how her father stood back, though. He had always seemed to know that things weren't perfect in her first marriage and she went to his side. "I'm happy about this, Poppi."

He gave her a long level stare. "That's the important thing."

He kissed her forehead but didn't move toward Derek. Instead Derek came over to her father and held his hand out to the other man.

Her father reluctantly reached for it and shook it.

"I know that I have to prove to you that I'm good enough for your only daughter, Mr. Velasquez, and I promise over time I will make that happen."

Bianca was fooled by the sincerity in his voice. And she wondered at the ease with which Derek was making these promises. First to Beni and now to her dad. She wondered if he thought that this would go beyond temporary or if he had a way out of this for them both that would keep the peace between their families.

For her sake she needed everything between herself and Derek to be the truth. They were lying to their families, to the town, to everyone outside of each other so in order to keep herself in check, she needed to always remember that truth when she looked at him. And his promises were making it a little hard to remember this was temporary.

Nine

Derek pulled her into his arms as the music turned from Pitbull to Ed Sheeran and "Tenerife Sea." He didn't think too much about the lyrics, but just enjoyed holding Bianca in his arms. Beni and Penny had gone home with their grandparents and his brothers, Kinley, Ferrin and Pippa were still here along with Diego, Inigo and Rowdy. Pippa was dancing with Diego, which didn't seem like the best idea since he knew that Diego was a player and that Pippa had secrets she wasn't sharing.

The other guys were in the house either watching basketball on the big screen or playing cards. Since

Ethan was at the table and dealing, Derek was very glad he was out here on the courtyard dancing with Bianca. His brother was a card shark and very good at winning.

"So you're making a lot of very convincing promises to Beni, to my father…you thinking something you haven't mentioned to me?" she asked.

He cursed under his breath as he danced her away from the other couples and then rested his forehead against hers and looked down into her eyes. "I think even if this is pretend, we need to make it look real. And any man who is going to try to claim you, Bianca, has to know that your father doesn't give his approval easily. Did he and Jose get on?"

She tightened her mouth and he wondered if he'd asked something he shouldn't, but he'd never been one of those guys to tiptoe around the uncomfortable questions. And tonight more than any other he needed to know what he was up against.

Because Bianca had just echoed the same sentiment that Ethan had expressed earlier. He had been making this real. Too real. And he'd already dismissed the excuse he'd been giving himself that it was okay to do this because she'd been his crush back in the day. He knew that she was so much more to him than that now. But he was supposed to be easing himself into her life.

Not throwing a party like this, he thought. One

that left no doubt that he wanted this to last. Which was why she was questioning him and why he'd got his back up and asked her about Jose.

Jose was the one man that Derek would never be able to compete with. The guy was dead. The guy had fathered her son. The guy had been more at ease with romantic gestures than Derek ever would be.

He could only ever be a pale imitation.

Damn.

Screw that.

He imitated no one.

He was the best there was in Cole's Hill and pretty much in the top 1 percent in the country when it came to heart surgeons. He didn't live in the shadows.

And he wasn't prepared to with Bianca, either.

"Jose and my dad didn't get along. At first they seemed to be fine but then...well, about the time I got pregnant something happened and he and Dad stopped being chummy."

"What happened?"

She took a deep breath, looked around the courtyard and then grasped his hand, drawing him toward the glass doors right in front of them. Opening them, she stepped inside with Derek close behind. He knew she hadn't realized the doors led to his bedroom.

She glanced around and flushed.

"I just wanted to be alone."

"It's okay. I'm not planning on sweeping you off your feet and onto my bed…yet," he said with a wink. "I want to hear what happened first."

"It's…embarrassing, really."

"I doubt it," he said.

"No, it is. You know how we had that big wedding with all the cameras and media coverage and how everyone thought we were the romantic fairy-tale couple of the decade?"

He nodded, not really sure he wanted to hear this.

"Well, I thought we were, too. I was deeply in love with him and I couldn't see any faults. Marco Moretti, the head of the Moretti Motors Racing Team, and his wife tried to warn me that Jose was all show."

"Why did they try to warn you?"

"We are good friends. The team travels from country to country and some of the families go along, but I was an outsider and because of the modeling I'd done some of the other wives and girlfriends didn't welcome me. But Virginia, Marco's wife, did. Anyway, one day I was going on about how great Jose was and she said to be careful not to buy into that effortless charm he had with women."

Derek felt a stone in his stomach as he started putting things together. Little things she'd said and the way she'd reacted when Derek had mentioned her late husband. He realized that Jose had been a player.

"It's okay. You don't have to say anything else. I'm not going to cheat on you," he said.

"I know you won't, Derek. This is for three months. That's the part that I'm struggling with. You know? I'm beginning to think it's my fatal flaw. That I fall for guys who are just putting on a show. And this show…it's hard not to fall for it.

"I think Dad is reserving judgment on you until he can be sure you're the guy you claim to be," Bianca said at last.

He was. And he wasn't. He'd thought they would do each other a favor. They'd both get something they wanted and then life would go back to the way it had been. But having kissed her and seen beyond the image of who Bianca was, he knew they never could.

And he didn't want to hurt her the way that Jose had. He didn't want to put another black cloud over her dreams. He wanted to tell her that maybe this wouldn't be temporary, but he didn't know that himself. Promising to be there for Beni had been easy. But promising her father not to hurt her might have been more than he could deliver. Making a promise to Bianca…he couldn't do that until he knew if he could handle both her and his career.

Nothing had ever competed with surgery for his attention. He'd dated but all of those relationships hadn't drawn him away from medicine the way he feared Bianca could.

* * *

She'd said too much; she knew it but it was time to clear the air. Now that their families knew about this engagement there was no changing her mind. Not that she'd really considered it but the time had definitely passed.

"Sorry. I shouldn't have mentioned that," she said, glancing around Derek's room. A lamp on one of the bedside tables was turned on, casting a soft glow around the room. It was large, with a king-size bed against one wall. There was a treadmill facing a flat-screen TV mounted on the wall next to the dresser. A seating area took up most of the opposite side of the room and there was a door that she assumed led to a private bath.

"Your room is interesting," she said.

He walked farther into the room to lean against the dresser. He had his long legs stretched out in front of him and then crossed his arms over his chest. He watched her with that enigmatic Derek stare. The one that she could never read.

"In what way?"

"Just very utilitarian," she said as she walked over to the seating area and noticed the bookshelf behind it. She scanned the titles: not a single work of fiction but a lot of medical journals.

"It's comfortable."

"I can see that," she said.

"You sound like you don't approve," he said, getting up to walk toward her.

She plopped down on one of the overstuffed leather armchairs and reached for the book that was on the side table between the chairs.

"This would put me straight to sleep."

"Are you sure?" he asked, taking the book from her. "It's about an experimental procedure for heart valve stents that has had some limited success. I'm thinking about possibly going to visit with the doctors who did the research to see some of their patients. If it works it would be an improvement on the operation we are using now."

There was that intensity that she'd always noticed in him when he talked about medicine. Any other guy would be trying to bum-rush her into bed and Derek was telling her why the book he was reading was interesting. It made her heart beat a little faster. She liked it when he got all serious and doctorly. "Why can't you just try it here?"

"It's risky. And some of the facts seem off to me. I want to see the actual research."

"Off how?"

"Some of the numbers and ratios don't add up," he said, tossing the book on the table. "But that's boring. I have exciting things in the room, too."

She glanced around it and then pointed to the treadmill. "The exercise equipment?"

He shook his head.

"Do you have sex toys in your dresser?" she asked with a wink. "I've read *Fifty Shades of Grey.*"

"Hell, no. I don't need toys to please you," he said.

She flushed and cleared her throat, which was suddenly very dry. And now all she could think about was that big bed and him pleasing her.

She tried to push the images of his naked body moving over hers out of her mind but she couldn't. She had seen him at the pool and knew his chest was solid and muscly but now she wondered what it would feel like under her fingers. Did he have hair on his chest? She couldn't remember.

He arched one eyebrow at her.

"What?"

"I think you just realized the most thrilling thing in my room is me."

She shook her head. "That's a lot of talk, Caruthers."

"Again, with you thinking it's all ego. I promise you it's fact," he said.

"Another promise?" she asked.

"This one I'm happy to demonstrate," he said. "Remember that kiss by the lake?"

"I've thought of little else," she said. "I know that temporary means that we should keep our distance."

Derek stood up and drew her to her feet next to him. "Don't think. No more second-guessing any of this. Let's just see where it leads."

She bit her lip. She couldn't agree to that. They had a deal and she didn't want to shirk her side of it. "Do you mean that you want this to go beyond the three months?"

"I just mean let's take it slow and easy."

"That's not exactly an answer," she said. "I can't 'go with the flow.' I'm a single mom."

"You're an engaged woman who is in her fiancé's arms."

Bianca didn't really think she was, though. She felt those lies of fake and temporary weighing heavily on her and despite the fact that this was Derek and she wanted him more than she had wanted any man in a long time, she wedged her arm between them and stepped back.

"I'm not. This already feels way too damned real and it's not. I see this room and you are a surgeon first, Derek," she said. "There's a reason why you asked me to be your fiancée and it's not because you are waiting for the right woman. It's because no woman can compete with your career. I would love to go with the flow and if I was four years younger then I'd give in. But I'm not. I'm the woman that life has made me. I'm Benito's mom. I have to look beyond what feels good. I have to do what is right."

She hadn't meant to get so real with him but it needed to be said. She couldn't read him. She didn't know if he was faking this or if he thought that lust was enough for them. That an affair would be fine since they knew they'd be going back to their real lives in a few months. But she had already realized that she was in danger of believing every bit of this. And sleeping with Derek wasn't going to help her remember that he wasn't really hers.

The truth in her words cut through the thick lies he'd been telling himself. And it underscored the reasons why he'd been reluctant to make any more promises to Bianca. He had no idea if he could commit to a woman—even her—for more than three months. That was what he'd sort of been implying when he'd asked her to go along with it for now.

But Bianca wasn't that kind of woman.

She wasn't one who could be coaxed into half measures. He knew the reasons for her wariness were well-founded. He'd cut her off earlier because he didn't want her to say it out loud but he suspected she'd been about to tell him that Jose had hooked up with other women when he was married to Bianca bothered Derek. It made him mad as hell and want to find the guy and punch him.

But Jose was dead.

Derek hated him. He was glad that the man was out of Bianca's life but he was angry that he hadn't realized before now that she'd had such a crappy marriage. They'd been friends. Surely, Derek should have noticed.

But what would he have done?

That guy had done a job on Bianca and now he was gone. Maybe she felt relief or sadness… Oh, hell, what if she still loved him? Maybe that was the real reason for the failed blind dates set up by her mother and her agreement to this…idea that was seeming more and more complicated by the minute. He wanted it to be simple again. The way it had been when he'd first conceived it. But he knew that it would never be simple.

What had started out with the best of intentions was now making his gut ache. He wanted her. That was a given. They were young, good-looking and there'd always been a sort of what-could-have-been vibe between them. But now that he was alone with her in his bedroom, he knew he didn't want her to leave.

That even though they'd never discussed it he didn't want their arrangement to be platonic.

"I get that. But there is something more going on between us, Bia. And there always has been," he said. "Do you deny it?"

She shrugged.

"No. You can't get off that easily. I need an answer. If this is just coming from me that's one thing, but when we kissed by the lake the other night something stirred between us. Or was it just me?" he asked.

Three days. It seemed hard to believe that it had only been three days since he'd asked her to be his fiancée because he'd changed in that time. It was inevitable, he thought. They'd always been close and she was one of the few people who'd seen past his nerdy façade to the man beneath. She was special.

But right now he wasn't sure if most of those feelings should have stayed in the past.

"There is something between us. But I don't want to be a fool again. Love and me are adversaries. The last time I thought it was real, it wasn't. This time… I know it's fake. I know we are playing house to get you that chief of cardiology position and give me some breathing room to figure out what's next. But tonight felt real. And this ring…it's not a ring you give a fake fiancée."

He put his hand under her chin and tipped her head back until their eyes met. She'd kicked her heels off earlier when the dancing had started and was back to her normal five-foot, seven-inch height, which meant he towered over her in bare feet.

There were clouds in her eyes and fear as well. And he knew the pain of being hurt. Not of being in love, because he was honest enough to admit he'd been careful about his relationships and never pursued one with a woman who could touch him as deeply as Bianca. But he had been hurt.

He started to open his mouth. To make vows that he had no idea if he could keep or not. He wanted to say he'd never hurt her.

But he wasn't sure whether he was going to hurt himself.

"I… If I said this was a temporary affair, would that make it easier? I think we'd be fooling ourselves if we said we aren't going to sleep together," he finally said.

When he was unsure he always fell back on the bluntness that he'd used in his early residency days. It was just easier to detach when he was blunt. If she said no, it was fine. He'd wanted women before and not slept with them. But of course, they hadn't been living with him.

And she would be.

With her son, who was already starting to make Derek care for him. And with her swarm of brothers, who would probably beat him to a pulp if he hurt their sister. Two of her brothers lived in the Five Families neighborhood and the other two on the family's ranch.

"Maybe. I'm not trying to make this harder than it has to be. It's just that I seem to have the worst instincts when it comes to men. I really thought that since you were such a good friend this wouldn't happen."

"Really?" he asked, a tad disappointed.

She sighed, then shook her head. "No. Since I've been back in Cole's Hill, I have noticed you."

"What can I do to make this work?" he asked. "Drop the fake engagement? Sleep with you? Avoid sleeping with you?"

"I don't know. It would be so much easier if there was a crystal ball we could look into and see the future."

"It would be. Barring that, I think we should return to my suggestion that we sort of just see where this leads. We've been friends for as long as I can remember. I really don't want to think that I've done something that will lead to me losing you."

"I don't want that, either," she said. "Should we get back to our guests?"

"I don't think they'll miss us."

In the distance he heard the music change again. This time to Blake Shelton's "Sangria." He pulled her close and rocked them back and forth to the music. Her arms slipped around his waist and her hands held him tight. She sang under her breath and for now he told himself this was enough.

Ten

Derek moved to the music and she knew that they should leave his bedroom. But being in here all alone made her feel safe. She was in his arms and she felt like she'd found a man she could trust. With her heart and her body. She knew it might be the sangria she'd drunk at dinner or just the fact that he'd given her an heirloom ring. She couldn't put her finger on it but she knew once she left this bedroom she wasn't going to allow herself to be vulnerable around him again.

She had this night.

This chance to be with him.

She opened her eyes and saw he was looking

down at her with intent. She tipped her head to the side and ran her fingers through that thick curly hair of his, pushing it to the left the way he liked to. His hair was silky and soft.

He moaned, the sound coming from deep inside of him, and he traced her fingers down over the side of his face and around his ear and then down his neck. She felt his pulse and as she kept touching him it started to speed up a little.

She raised both eyebrows at him, a slight smile playing on her lips. "Like that?"

"Hell, yes," he said, lifting his hand to rub his thumb over the pulse on her neck. He just slowly caressed her, moving his finger back and forth.

Shivers spread from where he was touching her over her collarbone and down her arms. Her breasts felt full and her nipples tingled.

"Like that?" he asked.

"Yes," she said, her voice breathy to her own ears.

He moved his hand to cup her neck and the back of her head. His fingers tangled in her hair and slowly drew her head back as he lowered his. Their lips met and an electric current made her lips buzz.

He parted his and she felt his breath and then the brush of his tongue. He thrust it into her mouth and their tongues tangled. Twisting her fingers into his hair, she held him to her so he didn't change his mind and pull back.

He anchored her body to his with one hand on her waist and the other one in her hair, holding her while he ravaged her mouth. She felt his erection thickening against her lower stomach and she shifted, rubbing herself against him.

He ran one of his hands down her arm, slowly and lightly caressing the outside of her arm, and then drew his hand back up the inside, the backs of his fingers brushing the side of her breast. It had been so long since a man had touched her that she realized that common sense had nothing to do with this.

She had felt empty and so undesirable for too long. And now Derek was holding her. Kissing her like he never wanted to stop as she shifted her hips, gyrating against him. Her eyes were closed, but there was no doubt of who was touching her. His cologne—spicy and masculine—perfumed each breath she took. His touch was precise, his hands sure.

He wrapped one arm around her hips and lifted her off her feet. He carried her across the room and then carefully laid her down on the bed, coming down on top of her. One of his legs bent to fall next to her on the bed while the other stayed between her spread legs.

She let go of him, her arms falling out to the side as she looked up at him and felt the emotion of the moment.

Tears burned the back of her eyes and she felt stupid because this was Derek and he was so sweet and caring and she wanted this to be real.

Oh, damn. Double damn. Just do the physical thing, she told herself. Forget emotions. They couldn't be trusted anyway.

But Derek wasn't Jose and he noticed immediately. He came down on the bed by her side and pulled her into his arms, rubbing one of his hands down her back. The other one wiped away the hot tears that fell on her face.

"What is it?"

She shook her head. She didn't want him to know how long it had been since she'd had sex. Or that she had felt ugly and unfeminine after she'd given birth and Jose had pushed her away.

All the baggage she'd thought she'd stowed in a locker and buried deep inside of her soul was coming to the surface.

"It's been a long time for me," she said.

He gazed at her, those blue eyes of his full of an emotion that looked a lot like caring. She stopped analyzing and expecting to be hurt and decided to take Derek at face value.

"Sorry. It's just that after I had the baby it took me a while to get into shape and it affected my sex life with Jose. Wow, that's a mood killer, isn't it," she said. "What kind of man wants to hear about this kind of crap?"

"Me. Listen, I'm sorry you had a horrible time with Jose. But I'm not him and I would never hurt you. You are the sexiest woman I've ever seen. I have been crushing on you since I was fourteen."

"Fourteen?"

"Yeah."

"You should know I don't look like that poster of Jessica Simpson in that Daisy Duke getup you used to have in your locker," she said. "I'm real and not airbrushed."

"Good. I like real. I like you, Bianca. I want to make love to you," he said. "But I have no agenda here. If we don't tonight then it will happen when it's meant to."

"I'm afraid if I walk out of here tonight I'll do everything in my power to keep my distance from you."

"I can be pretty damned determined. And we're going to live together," he said. "Trust me—when the time is right it will happen."

Derek hadn't meant for things to heat up. She'd led them into his bedroom and then gotten way too real. But now that he had her in his arms and on his bed the urgency was there, of course, but he had long ago learned to control it. Control was everything to a surgeon and he applied it to every aspect of his life.

He shifted them until they were lying with their heads at the top of the bed. He piled the pillows behind his back and held her close to his side. She wasn't talking and that was okay with him as she kept running her hands over his chest. She slipped her finger between the buttons of his shirt and he had the first inkling that she didn't want this night to end.

But he waited.

She'd cried when he'd laid her on his bed. Any man worth his salt would know that things were going to take time.

"What are you doing?" he asked as he felt her nail scrape over the skin under his shirt.

"Touching you. Do you like it?"

"Yeah," he said. "Want me to take my shirt off?"

She sat up and turned away, only to look over her shoulder at him. She had a tentative expression on her face but she nodded. "Do you mind?"

"Not at all. You know what a big ego I have, so having a woman admire my body just feeds it."

She turned back to him and fake-punched him. "Don't be an ass."

"I'm not. Figured I'd beat you to saying it," he said with a wink. Then he tugged the tails of his shirt out of his pants and slowly undid the buttons. Not because he was trying to be coy but because his hands were shaking.

His surgeon's hands were shaking because Bianca Velasquez had asked him to take his shirt off. He'd pretty much already told himself that he was going to go slow with her. And every instinct in his body wanted to do the exact opposite. But he wasn't about to rush her or make her uncomfortable. It seemed to him as though she'd had enough of that in her marriage.

When he had his shirt unbuttoned she put her hand in the center of his chest. "I couldn't remember if you had a hairy chest or not."

"Just a little bit. Does that bother you?" he asked. One of the women he'd dated had wanted him to wax his chest, which had been the end of that relationship. But if Bianca asked…well, he'd consider it.

"No. I like it. I like the way it feels against my fingers when I do this," she said, rubbing her hand over his pectorals. She spread her fingers wide, the tip of one brushing over his nipple, which felt odd. He didn't really like it and brought his hand over hers to move it off.

She tugged her hand free and traced the hair from his chest along the narrow trail down his stomach. She stopped when she reached his waistband, running her fingernail along the edge. He had to shift his legs to accommodate his burgeoning erection. She noticed and ran her hand over it, stroking him up and down through the fabric of his trousers.

It was the most delicate torture to have her touching him. "I'd like to try this again."

"Now?" he asked.

"Yes," she said.

"Then come over here and kiss me," he said. She kept her hand on his erection and inched upward until she lay curved against his side. He lowered his head and kissed her. He kept the kisses as controlled as he could. He wanted to be ready to stop if she asked him to.

And that was going to be difficult because everything in him wanted to claim her. Wanted to make love to her and really make her his, so that she wasn't just his as far as everyone was concerned but the two of them would know she was his as well.

He skimmed his hands lightly over her side and when he reached the slit of her dress, he groaned. Her skin was soft, smooth and warm. He ran his finger along the edge of the fabric and then slowly inched it underneath around to her back to cup her buttocks in his hand and draw her closer to him. Then he moved her up and over his body.

She sucked his tongue deeper into her mouth and his penis jumped under her hand. She undid his zipper and slipped her hand into his pants, finding the opening in his boxers. Her fingers were long and cool against his erection. He felt his control slowly slipping away but he clung to it.

He reached for the zipper at the back of her dress and lowered it slowly. He was giving her time to say no if she wanted to but she sat up and rolled off the bed, standing up to take her dress off. It fell in a pool on the floor and he sat up to more fully see her.

She wore a balconette bra that pushed her breasts up and created a deep cleavage. He skimmed his gaze down her body, to the nipped-in waist, to her hips. She wore a tiny pair of bikini underwear in a nude color.

She held her arms out to her sides.

"This is me," she said.

He crawled across the bed and sat on the edge of it in front of her. Putting his hands on her waist, he drew her closer to him. He kissed her stomach and then her ribs and slowly worked his way over her entire torso. She was gorgeous. She was Bianca, and he had never seen a woman he wanted more.

"You're lovely."

"I think you're punch-drunk," she said. "But very nice."

"I'm not nice. I'm one big egomaniac, remember?" he said, drawing her down on his lap. She straddled him, wrapping her arms around his shoulders and pushing her fingers into his hair again.

She'd done that a number of times. She must like his hair, he thought. But really he was grasping onto any thought to distract himself from how good she felt in his arms. He told himself he'd take it slow. That he wasn't going to rush or pressure her. She was hard to resist but he did it.

He leaned forward to kiss the top of the globes of her breasts. They were full and creamy-looking in the muted light from his bedside lamp. He used his tongue to trace the lacey pattern of the bra that hugged her breasts and then wrapped his arms behind her back and undid the clasp.

She shifted around on his lap, pulling the fabric free from her body and tossing it on the floor. Her breasts were full and her nipples were pointed little nubs. He rubbed his finger over them as her hands moved lower on his body.

He felt her fingers fumbling for the button at his waistband. He stopped her before she went any further. "Are you sure about this? I think I could stop right now but if you take my pants off…"

"I'm sure. It was just…leftovers from my former life. I hadn't realized how much of myself I'd lost until now. In a way, you helped me, Derek," she said.

"Good. I'm glad to hear it," he replied. "One more thing."

"Yes?"

"Are you on the pill?"

She blushed; the color started at her breasts and went up to her cheeks. "No. I didn't even think… I'm not really that active."

"It's okay, I've got condoms."

"Good. I don't want to stop," she said.

"Me, either. Wrap your arms and legs around me," he said.

She did and he stood up, set her down on the bed and then turned away to take off his pants and boxers. He reached into the nightstand and took out one of the condoms he kept there.

He felt the brush of her fingers along his back and turned to look at Bianca. She was touching the scarred flesh on his left side.

"Was this from the car-surfing incident?" she asked.

He nodded. During his early teenage years he'd been eager to prove himself as brave as his brothers and had earned a reputation for never turning down a dare. So he'd ended up on his skateboard being towed behind one of his friend's older brother's cars. But he'd slipped off and been dragged along for a few feet.

"Yes. Being dragged along asphalt leaves its mark."

"I'm sorry you were hurt. I remember when I came to visit you at the ranch and your father said that dum-dums shouldn't have pretty visitors."

"Always so eloquent. But he was both pissed and worried. Not a great combination for him."

She ran he fingers lower to Derek's hip bone and then reached around to his front and took his erection in her hand again. She ran her fingers down his length and he turned to face her.

She smiled up at him and scooted back on the bed. He noticed she'd taken her panties off and was completely naked. His breath caught and all of the control he'd always taken for granted deserted him as he came down on the bed on top of her.

He needed to be inside her now. This was Bianca, the one woman he'd wanted above all others for longer than he could remember. He parted her thighs as he rubbed his chest over the tips of her breasts. She wrapped her legs around his waist and he felt the tip of his erection at the entrance of her body.

He cursed.

"What?"

"Condom. I forgot to put it on," he said.

She took it from him and as he shifted to his knees she tore the packet open and put the condom on him. Then she took his length in her hand and drew him forward.

He groaned. Putting his hands on the bed on either side of her body, he fell forward until he could trace her nipple with his tongue.

Now she moaned as she wrapped her legs around his waist again. He found her entrance and lifted his head to look up at her. He wanted to see the moment when he entered her.

Taking her hands in his and stretching them up over her head, he slowly pushed into her body. She was so tight he thought he wasn't going to make it all the way in before he came.

But soon he was buried hilt-deep in her body. Her hands tightened on his, her head rolled back and her eyes slowly shut.

He began to thrust into her, drawing out and then pushing back in. She clutched at his hips as he started, holding him to her, eyes half-closed and head tipped back.

He leaned down and caught one of her nipples in his teeth, scraping very gently. She started to tighten around him. Her hips were moving faster, demanding more, but he kept the pace slow, steady, wanting her to come again before he did.

He suckled her nipple and rotated his hips to catch her pleasure point with each thrust. Then he felt her hands clenching in his hair as she threw her head back and her climax ripped through her.

He started to thrust faster. He tipped her hips up to give him deeper access to her body. She was still clenching around his when he felt that tightening at the base of his spine seconds before his body erupted into hers. He pounded into her two, three more times, then collapsed against her. Careful to keep his weight from crushing her, he rolled to his side, taking her with him.

He kept his head at her breast and smoothed his hands down her back. He finally lifted his head as his breathing slowed and looked up at her to make sure she was all right. She smiled down at him. He held her close in the curve of his body and drew the edge of the comforter over them.

He might have started this as a reason to keep an old girlfriend off his back but as of tonight, he knew that he'd found a woman he wanted to keep. Now and forever.

Something that was underscored when they both got dressed and went back out to the party. She seemed to sparkle as she moved through their guests and occasionally glanced over at him with a secret smile.

He felt more daring than he had when he'd car surfed and he knew that it was because of her. Bianca.

A woman who held more power over him than he realized he had given to her.

Eleven

Bianca woke up in a strange room wrapped in Derek's arms. She carefully got out of the bed and looked back at him sleeping there. The music had long since stopped and the house was quiet. She glanced at the nightstand clock and saw that it was almost 3:00 a.m.

If she'd had any doubts that Derek was a special man to her, they were all gone now. And the word *temporary* had been shoved so far to the back of her mind that she was trying to figure out how to move forward. She knew there had to be a way.

She just had to figure it out.

Derek stirred on the bed and sat up, the comforter falling to his waist. He scrubbed his hand over his eyes and then looked at her.

"You okay?"

She nodded. "I… I need the bathroom and to wash this makeup off my face."

"Mind if I join you in there?" he asked. "Sorry for conking out on you like that."

"It's okay. I did the same," she said. "Let me pee first and then you can come in."

"Fair enough. I can use one of the bathrooms down the hall," he said.

"Nah. Give me a sec," she said, walking to the adjoining bathroom. Then she paused in the doorway and when she looked back, she noticed his eyes were on her butt.

"Do you have a T-shirt I can borrow?"

"Yeah," he said.

She hurried into the bathroom and did her business, calling out when she was done that he could come and join her. Derek had some decent face soap that was fragrance-free so it didn't irritate her skin. He came in and handed her a T-shirt printed with the San Antonio Spurs logo. She put it on.

It was a master bathroom that had two sinks. She went to the one that was clearly not being used by Derek. His toothbrush and razor were next to the other one.

She braided her hair into two plaits to keep it out of the water and then started to wash her face as Derek washed up as well.

"So…you okay?" he asked, his voice casual.

As she was drying her face on the towel he'd handed her, she remembered how unsure she'd been when she'd first come into his bedroom last night. And how she'd been crying.

The sex was…what needed to happen.

She lowered the towel and looked at him.

"Actually I'm pretty good. Thanks for that. I needed it."

He gave her the biggest, cockiest grin she'd ever seen from him. "Me, too."

She couldn't help it: she started laughing. She felt young and free in this moment, something that she'd lost somewhere in the last few years. There were moments when she held her son that she approached that feeling but it was nothing like this.

He started to walk toward her when his phone buzzed loudly from the next room.

"Crap," he said, brushing past her and stalking into the bedroom.

Her lover was gone and in his place was the surgeon. She'd seen him give a lecture at the hospital a few months ago when she'd attended a charity function and had been impressed by the difference in the personal and professional sides of the man she knew.

Derek was by nature a bit of a charming rogue but when he was focused on his career he was intense and there was no time for frivolity.

He had that same intensity and focus speaking on his phone when she walked back into the bedroom. His questions were quick-fire and he had gone to his closet and started pulling out clothes. She realized he was going to have to go work.

It was three…in the morning.

This was something she hadn't considered. Derek tossed her a pair of basketball shorts with a draw-string waist and she drew them on. He was going to have to leave pretty quickly. Staying in his house alone wasn't what she wanted so she started gathering up her dress and clothes. Her purse was in the foyer on a table. By the time he was off the phone she thought she'd gotten everything.

"I have to go to the hospital," he said. "Sorry I don't have time to talk about it. Want me to drop you off at your parents' house?"

"Yes, please. Do you have time? I can walk," she said.

"I'll take you. The patient is en route to the hospital so I have a few moments to spare but we have to leave now."

He led the way through the darkened house. She grabbed her bag as he opened the front door. He had them in the car in a moment. Though he wasn't talking, she had a chance to see him in full-on doctor mode. She saw that he was already thinking about the upcoming surgery. He received an email and called the attachment up on the in-dash screen. It looked like an X-ray.

He pulled up in front her parents' house and she reached for the door handle but he leaned over and kissed her, hard and deep. "Sorry about this."

"It's your job," she said. "We can talk tomorrow."

"Yes," he said.

She let herself into the house and heard Derek speed away. She quietly made her way up to her room, dropping off her clothes before poking her head into Benito's room to check on him. He was sleeping with his mouth open. She stood over him and watched him for a few minutes before going back into her own room.

She took off the shorts that Derek had loaned her but left the tee on. She reached for her cell phone, which she'd left charging on her nightstand, and texted him to say good luck with his surgery.

She was surprised when she noticed the three dancing dots that signaled he was responding.

Thank you. Sorry the night had to end so soon. Looking forward to living with you.

Bianca quickly typed her reply.

Me, too.

She put the phone away and tried to go to sleep but her mind was buzzing. As she drifted off, she remembered the feel of Derek's arms around her, the Ed Sheeran song playing in the background of her mind.

Derek met Raine in the presurgery room where they scrubbed up. She briefed him on the additional information that the EMTs had sent on their way in. They were going straight into the operating room as the patient had shown all the symptoms of a heart attack and had undergone ten minutes of CPR and was failing. They'd finally revived him enough for surgery.

He worked carefully for the next six hours and when they emerged he knew he'd done all he could to save the patient. And it looked like the man was going to survive; Derek was cautiously optimistic. After cleaning up, he looked for Raine but she was with the family. Despite his exhaustion, his mind was buzzing from the surgery. He mentally reviewed every cut he'd made. Which was why he was distracted when he entered the lounge and bumped into someone who was standing there.

Looking up, he was surprised to see Marnie.

"You look tired," she said.

"I am. Surgery does that," he said. He wasn't being curt; his mind just wasn't back to functioning in the real world. He was still going over everything he'd done. He knew he'd done the best he could with a heart that was badly damaged.

"This was one of the things I hated about dating you," she said. "I thought if I worked at the hospital it would help me understand you. But I'm not sure it does."

He looked at Marnie. She'd done something different with her makeup today and she seemed softer. He walked over to the coffeepot and poured himself a cup. He had rounds and then he'd be able to head home and catch some sleep.

"I'm sure it doesn't. It's for the best that we're not together," he said.

"I heard about your fiancée this morning. Bianca Velasquez…very impressive," Marnie said.

"She is. We've been friends for a long time. She knew me before I was a surgeon."

"That might help her. Well, I hope it lasts," Marnie said.

Derek didn't know how to respond to that. "Why wouldn't it?"

"Because you aren't long on commitment," Marnie said. "Remember you started to get itchy about three days after we moved in together."

He wanted to tell her that it was all the junk she'd

brought and the schedule she'd put on the fridge. How they both had to check in constantly with each other. But he held his tongue. There was no reason to start an argument with her. She was out of his life and they were both in a better place now.

"It feels different this time," he said.

She looked hurt and he realized that his words might have stung her. "We just weren't a good fit, Marn. You know it and I know it."

"I've changed," she said softly.

"I haven't," he said. "I've got rounds but I'll see you on Wednesday for the board meeting. Have a good Saturday."

He walked out of the room before she said anything else. The board was meeting every week for updates on the progress of the new cardio wing. He would be attending, and there would be no way to avoid her.

His encounter with Marnie made him miss Bianca. It was almost ten in the morning and he did have rounds to make but he pulled out his phone and texted her, and they began a back-and-forth.

Good morning. You awake yet?

I have a toddler. I've been awake since five.

Ouch. I have rounds but maybe this afternoon you and Beni can come over and start planning the move in.

I'd like that. I just got an email asking me to come to Manhattan on Tuesday for a photo shoot. I was thinking of going. Mom and Dad will watch Beni.

Should I wait until I get back to move in?

No. I think you should get settled this weekend.

Derek didn't want her to leave. He wanted them to get settled into living together. And he hated to admit that now part of it was about proving Marnie wrong about his ability to live with a woman. But he knew that he couldn't ask Bianca to not take a job. He'd never have stayed home this morning if she'd asked.

He knew surgery and modeling were different careers but hers was just as important as his.

OK. I'll take you to the airport.

Thanks. Text me when you want us to come over.

:) See ya later.

He pocketed his phone and finished his rounds, including a visit to the patient he'd done emergency surgery on overnight. Derek was pleased to see that he was responding well. He talked to the family and then left the hospital.

He drove home. As soon as he went inside, he headed to his bedroom. He could smell Bianca's perfume and saw the rumpled sheets that reminded him of last night. And there was an emptiness inside him as he looked around the house.

He wanted Bianca here. He needed her here in his house. Marnie had been right when she'd said that he hadn't been able to live with her. But Bianca was different. He took a quick nap, showered and then texted her that he was ready for her and Beni to start moving their stuff in.

He offered to pick her up but she said she was going to bring her own car.

He told himself that this was just a normal afternoon but he felt like a kid getting ready to go to bed on Christmas Eve. He was full of anticipation but when the doorbell rang he forced himself to walk slowly toward the door.

"Hello," he said opening the door.

"Hiya, Derry," Benito said.

He smiled down at her son, but his eyes never left Bianca's. There was something he saw there that made him believe that she had missed him, too.

He stepped back to let them enter, finally feeling like this house was about to become a home. And as much as that thrilled him he had to remember that he hadn't changed the parameters of their agreement.

Benito was pretty excited about having a "new dad." He'd talked of nothing else all morning and since his sentiment matched her mood she didn't say anything.

Derek looked tired but happy to see them. Cobie was in Houston visiting his girlfriend so it was just the three of them in the house.

"Beni, want to pick out your room?" Derek asked.

"Yes, Mama, you can have the room next to mine."

"Do you have any adjoining rooms?" she asked as Derek led the way to the stairs. In Texas, the master suites tended to be on the first floor and the other bedrooms and game rooms on the second floor.

One of the moms in Beni's playgroup had mentioned that not too long ago. Having grown up here it had seemed normal to Bianca but this mom who'd moved from Chicago had said her eight-year-old didn't like it and had been sleeping on the floor of her and her husband's bedroom every night. They were in the process of renovating the upstairs to accommodate the master suite.

She and Derek had slept together last night but she wasn't sure he'd planned on them moving into a room together. Besides they both were still trying to figure this out.

The notion that this was temporary had been put out of her mind but she had no idea if it had been for Derek as well. And it had only been one night. She knew…well, one night could change a lot of things but they hadn't talked so she had no idea where they stood.

Beni took her hand and then started singing a counting song as they went up the stairs. She sang along with him and noticed that Derek just followed behind. When they were all on the second floor, Beni dropped her hand to go explore the rooms.

"What was that?"

"Um…it's kind of embarrassing but I have a tendency to miss steps on the way down and slip on the stairs, so I count them as I walk down so I don't fall and Beni has always heard me because I really didn't want to fall when I was carrying him down the stairs. So when he learned the counting song at his day care he started singing it when we go up and down the stairs."

"I love it. You guys have a pretty close relationship," Derek said.

"We do. It's been mostly just he and I all of his life. He doesn't remember Jose that well. We have a lot of pictures of him and I tell Beni stories about his papa but it's hard." She paused before adding, "I think you should know he told *Abuelo* this morning that he has a new dad now."

Bianca wanted to make sure that Derek wasn't surprised in case Beni said anything to him. "I'll talk to him but he's small and so it's hard for him to understand that you are more like a friend."

"It's okay. We'll do it together."

She nodded. "I hope this isn't more than you intended when you asked me to do this."

"I think it already is," Derek said. "Things are changing but I have no regrets."

Hmm…well that didn't tell her anything. She wanted to pursue this topic further but maybe today wasn't the right time.

"How was surgery last night?" she asked.

"Good. The patient is responding well and I think he'll make a good recovery."

"I'm glad to hear that. I can't imagine what it's like to hold someone's life in your hands," she said. "I couldn't do it."

Derek stared at her for a long moment. "But you do it in a different way with Benito. And you do a wonderful job."

She was touched by his words and reached out to take his hand. "Thanks for saying that. But you haven't seen us in meltdown mode."

"I'm sure it's not as bad as you think."

"I'm going to let you keep believing that," she said.

Toddler-and-mom meltdowns weren't something that could be explained. They had to be seen to be believed. She and Beni were usually pretty good but sometimes he got tired and she got cranky. They weren't perfect.

"I think you should know that my track record with living with someone isn't the greatest," Derek said. "I… I'm not sure what I'll be like."

"I'm sure we'll be fine," she said, but that little dream she'd started to have about maybe making this permanent died a quick death. She didn't need a man, she knew that. Her happiness had never been dependent on one. But she liked Derek. She liked the idea of the two of them together.

She had bought into the advertising once again. She'd seen the party last night, experienced the tender lovemaking and thought, *This is it. This is real.*

The reason he hadn't expanded on what he'd said earlier was probably that he was still thinking that in three months they'd be out the door.

"Mama, I want this one," Beni said, poking his head out of one of the doorways.

Thank God for her little boy. She smiled at him and started down the hall. She was going to talk to him about Derek and she was going to have to make sure that even though they lived together she kept their lives separate. She already felt…well, like something had been taken from her but that was only an illusion.

She had wanted last night to be all physical and even though it hadn't been for her maybe it was good that it seemed to have been for Derek. She tried to reassure herself that it was much better to find out now before she allowed herself to care even more deeply for the man.

But the words rang hollow to her own ears and felt like a lie.

She smiled as Beni walked her around a room that connected to second one through a Jack-and-Jill bathroom.

She checked the room out and noticed the large walk-in closet. All the while, she tried to focus on the surroundings and not on the man who followed them quietly from room to room.

But that wasn't working.

Bianca had brought all of the stuff she'd been using at her parents' house over, mainly clothes, computers and Beni's favorite toys. Her brothers and Derek's had volunteered to get all of her stuff from storage so they were on their way.

The house was full of noise and men and Bianca wanted to hide out but she had to direct them as to where to put everything. Derek was helpful. She tried not to let it matter but he was so different from

Jose. It seemed to her that everything that had been fake with Jose was real with Derek and vice versa.

She hoped she was deluding herself and would snap out of it soon.

Twelve

A month went by in a blur.

Bianca had been to New York and Paris for modeling gigs. Benito had taken over the downstairs area with his books and playthings and Derek was starting to get used to seeing his toy F1 car parked in the courtyard. But sometimes that was all he saw of either of his houseguests.

And they were definitely houseguests. Something had changed the day after he'd made love to Bianca and by the time he'd realized it, it had felt too late to change it back. He was busy at the hospital and she was busy with her son and starting a lifestyle blog and video channel. Some days all he saw of her were the videos she posted.

He watched them and wanted her. But it also made him miss talking to her. But when he got home from the hospital she'd be at a family event or already in bed. It was hard to figure out how to get through to her and what he'd done to alienate her.

But today was the rehearsal dinner for Hunter's wedding to Ferrin so she couldn't avoid him any longer. They were staying in his old bedroom out at the Rockin' C together. Nate and Kinley had put them together and neither of them had wanted to say no, they couldn't share a room. Beni was having a sleepover in Penny's room. Pippa would be keeping an eye on the kids, including Conner, the son of Hunter's best friend, Kingsley. King and his new wife, Gabi were staying here as well. They were in town from California. The house was full of people and Derek hadn't seen his mom in such a good mood in a long time.

She'd hugged all of them more than once and kept saying how good it was to have all of her boys back on the ranch. It had made Derek realize that he should take more time to come and visit his parents.

He heard the bathroom door open and Bianca walked into the room wearing a jumpsuit with a halter neck that left her shoulders bare. The plunging neckline accentuated her cleavage. She had her hair up and her makeup was flawless as usual.

"I hadn't realized how big this party was going to be. I think there are going to be a few film crews here," Bianca said. "In case they ask about us, I'll try to downplay it. In fact, should I not even mention it?"

No.

"Definitely not. Listen, Bia, I'm not sure what I said to you that day we were picking out rooms in my house but this isn't going the way I wanted it to. Let's talk."

"Don't we have a party to get to?" she asked, going to the dresser and fiddling with her jewelry bag.

"No. Tonight is the first time we have been truly alone. I want to discuss this," he said.

"Well, I don't," she said. "I have enough on my mind as it is."

"Like what? My brother is the one getting married," he said.

"Like my marriage to Jose. This reminds me of it," she said, but he could tell it didn't. She was trying to come up with a reason not to talk to him.

"I'm sorry but that's not going to fly," Derek said. He went over to her, putting his hand on her shoulder while watching her in the mirror.

She looked up and in her eyes he saw…well, he wasn't sure if he was projecting his own feelings but it looked like sadness. Maybe she was really upset about the high-profile wedding.

He squeezed her shoulder. "We're friends. And we haven't been talking at all. If this is bothering you then tell me about it."

She turned to face him and he stepped back to give her some space because he knew she needed it.

"It's not the filming. It's just me. I've been in a funk lately," she said.

Derek hadn't noticed. He hadn't really seen her so it would be hard to notice her mood.

"What's up?"

She shrugged.

"Well, I've been a real douche at work. Raine told me if I don't come back from this weekend with a better attitude I was going to need to find a new assistant."

Bianca looked up at him then and for the first time in weeks he felt like she really saw him.

"Why?"

"Well, my best friend stopped talking to me and is avoiding me," he said.

"I thought Rowdy was your best friend," she said.

"Don't be coy. You know I mean you," he said. He walked closer to her. "I've missed you. I can't figure out what it was I did that set us on the path we're on."

She chewed her lower lip. "It wasn't really you. I was feeling unsure of how we should proceed and that day… I heard your warning. That you don't really like living with someone else. And I knew I had to be careful to keep our lives separate."

"Why?"

"Beni was already thinking of you as a 'new dad' and that can't be. Not if we are going to be going our own separate ways in a short amount of time. I wanted to make sure I didn't start to believe in something that you never meant for us to have."

Derek rubbed the back of his neck and turned away to keep from cursing out loud. He'd done this. He'd shoved her away to try to make sure that he didn't get hurt.

"That wasn't my intention," he said.

She watched him with those big brown eyes of hers that seemed to see all the way to his soul.

"What did you intend?" she asked.

He took a deep breath. He didn't know. In a way she'd given him exactly what he'd asked for, but it was hollow. Not what he wanted. But he hadn't realized that until he'd spent a month living with a woman he cared for.

"I intended to let you know that I wasn't sure what I was doing," he said. "I just wanted you to know I might screw up," Derek finally replied after a long pause.

"Why?"

"I'd seen Marnie at the hospital before I came home that day and she pointed out how much I hadn't enjoyed living with her. Seriously, after three days I was ready to throw all of her stuff out of the house or move into Nate's condo downtown instead."

Bianca had been dreading getting through this weekend, knowing she'd be so close to Derek and not have an easy way to escape him. This conversation was confirming her worst fears.

Since she'd moved into his house, she'd kept busy and hoped the feelings she had for him would disappear. That was something that happened with Jose once they'd been married.

But she realized the differences between the two men immediately. For one thing no matter how little contact they'd had every morning when she came downstairs she always found Derek's little notes on the counter telling her when he'd be home and wishing her a good day. He'd leave them alongside two glasses of pineapple juice, which he knew she and Beni drank each morning.

It was sweet.

It had been hard to figure out why he didn't like living with a woman, why he was avoiding her, when he did things like that. She'd just figured that maybe he was being polite, that he had wanted them to feel at home in his house. But the gestures didn't stop. One night she had to meet with her attorney in town and Derek had picked Beni up from his day care and brought him home. She'd come home to the two of them making tacos and Beni showing him how to do the salsa. Something his *abuela* in Spain had been teaching him.

It had been sweet but Bianca had faked a headache and gone upstairs to keep from…falling for Derek. He'd said one thing—but his actions had shown her something else.

But she had been afraid to trust her instincts. She'd been so wrong once before and falling for a man had made her…well, not the smartest girl in the world.

And as Bianca mulled over what he'd just said, she realized something she shouldn't have forgotten. They were both coming into this afraid of what the future might hold. Afraid of how they were going to move forward. She wanted to make this work. If the last month had shown her anything it was that even pretending he wasn't important in her life wasn't enough to actually keep her from falling for him.

She wondered how much of his treatment of her was a reaction to what living with Marnie had made him feel. She wasn't sure.

She wrapped her arms around her waist. If there was a scarier thing than falling for another person she had no idea what it was. There was no way to protect herself. She knew that. Because even reminding herself every morning that she had to keep her distance hadn't helped her to stop caring about Derek.

And she didn't just mean caring for him as a friend. She cared about him the way she would a lover. She missed him in her bed.

She missed talking to him at night. And it wasn't as if they'd even had that many conversations, which should give her a clue as to why she was falling for him. It was the quality of those conversations. Derek always listened to her and made her feel like she mattered. Something Jose had never done.

"I'm not Marnie," she said at last.

"Thank God. Listen, you know I'm not the best at saying the right thing. I don't want us to continue on the way we have been. I like you and Beni and I want us to do things together. Can we start over?"

Could they? They only had two months left on their arrangement. Would that be enough to show her what they could really be?

"Yes. But what exactly will we do?" she asked.

"You should stop avoiding me," he said. "I do love watching your videos but I'd rather see you in person."

"You've been watching my videos?" She felt a little thrill despite herself. "Do I look silly? Pippa suggested I try it. She said she's been watching a few of them for years and that they seem to make some good money. So I asked around when I was in Paris and there is money to be made. Plus I have a built-in brand," she said. "I'm rambling. Sorry, it's kind of unnerving to know someone I know has been watching the videos. Especially you."

"I missed you," he said at last. "I like talking to you and you were limiting us to notes on the counter."

"I thought that was what you wanted," she said. "By the way, I love your notes on the counter. Did Marnie hate that?"

She was a little jealous of the woman he'd lived with. For one thing, he hadn't been with Marnie because he needed a fake fiancée. But Bianca also wanted to know what was different about the two situations.

"I didn't do that with her. She used to wake me up in the morning so I could exercise with her. You know I use the treadmill and review cases and read up on experimental stuff, but when I said that to her, she took it to mean that I wanted more space…which made her immediately give me less."

Bianca had a feeling his relationship with the other woman wasn't as good as Marnie might have believed. "I am never going to wake you up to exercise. I'm fine with a dip in the pool in the morning and chasing Benito around in his little F1 car."

"Great. I don't want you to do anything different.

I think we should just stop avoiding each other and be ourselves," he said.

Someone knocked on the door.

"Yes?"

"Mom wants a picture of all of us boys and our women," Ethan said.

"Do you have a woman?" Derek asked, going to open the door.

Bianca followed him, trying not to let the fact that she was Derek's woman get to her too much. But it was exactly what she wanted to be. She was glad to know he'd been as dissatisfied with their arrangement as she had been. And that dream that she'd been trying to quash since she'd moved into his house suddenly seemed viable.

Her heart beat a little faster as she listened to Derek and his brother Ethan banter as they went downstairs.

Hunter and King were the life of the party. The best friends had lived for ten years under the cloud of suspicion of murdering Hunter's college girlfriend. Even though Hunter had been arrested and released without being charged, they'd been tried in the media and the damage was done. The scandal had followed them into the NFL and had even continued after their pro careers. It had only been last year when the murderer had been caught—an assistant coach on their college team who'd had a thing for drugging co-eds—and they both had been exonerated in the court of public opinion.

Derek, who'd watched his brother try to ignore the gossip for years, was glad to see him so happy. King had somehow gotten the microphone from the deejay at the party that had been set up in the backyard and was now telling stories about when he and Hunter had crashed a Superbowl party for their rivals. And Manu Barrett, the former NFL defensive lineman who was now a special teams coach on the West Coast, was joining in. Manu's brother was the astronaut Hemi Barrett who'd been chosen as part of the Cronus mission and trained outside of Cole's Hill on the Bar T land.

There were some TV cameras and a few video bloggers at the party. The crowd was a strange mix of college professors—Ferrin was an English professor at UT Austin—professional football players, astronauts, media folks, models, cardiologists, you name it. If Derek had one thought it was about how crazy his family was.

Ethan had been hanging back most of the night talking to Manu but once the defensive-lineman-turned-coach got up on the stage and started sharing football tales about Hunter's wild days, Ethan sought out Ferrin and whisked her away. Derek realized that his brother was trying to protect her from hearing any more stories about Hunter. All of them knew how hard Hunter had fallen for her and didn't want her to have second thoughts on marrying him.

"We need to get everyone dancing again," Derek said to Bianca.

"Agreed. Some of these stories should never have left the locker room. You go get the deejay to play something and I'll rally the guests. Have them play a song we can all dance to."

Derek left her and found the deejay but he had no idea what to request. He hadn't been to a "dance" that wasn't a charity event for the hospital or the Women's League in years. In fact the only song that came to mind was one he'd line-danced to back in middle school. But as soon as the music came on and he heard the laughter, he wasn't sure he'd made the right choice.

"'Macarena'? That's what you thought of?" Bianca asked as she took his hand and led him to the dance floor.

"I think the last time I was in charge of music was middle school."

She shook her head. "Well, it's working."

And it was. Everyone was laughing and dancing now and even all of Hunter's old teammates were on the floor. After the song was over they ended up dancing to "Gangnam Style." Watching a big former defensive lineman do that dance was one of the funniest things that Derek had ever seen. By the time they were doing the Electric Slide, everyone had forgotten about the stories that had been told about Hunter. Then the deejay slowed things down with a classic from Ella Fitzgerald that Ferrin had requested.

Derek pulled Bianca into his arms and slow-danced with her, noticing how all of his brothers were doing the same except for Ethan. Derek was glad he had Bianca. He was happy that he'd talked to her, too, because as the night progressed and the songs got slower and more sensual he realized he didn't want to be the only Caruthers besides Ethan on the outside watching this.

He wanted to be right where he was. In Bianca's arms. The last month had made him realize how much he wanted her in his life. Not temporarily, as he'd initially proposed, but for a long time.

He knew that he had one month, maybe two, to convince her that she wanted the same thing. And he didn't want to go overboard on her the way Marnie had with him. He didn't want to scare her off.

He held her close and his heart melted when she wrapped her arms around his waist and rested her head right over his heart. He was a heart surgeon; he knew that the organ didn't skip a beat or melt. But there was a part of him that would have sworn his heart did both of those things.

Soon they moved from dancing to drinking with his brothers and their friends. Bianca was sitting on his lap and she drifted to sleep while everyone was laughing and partying around them. It was time to call it a night.

Derek carried her up to his old bedroom and stood there watching her sleep. A part of him supposed he should go back out there with his brothers but he knew he didn't want to leave her. Finally he decided he should get her into something more comfortable.

He took off the halter top of her jumpsuit and then paused. He had no idea how to undress her without waking her up. And what if she did wake up and thought he was doing something…

"Derek?"

"Yes. I was trying to make you comfortable," he said. "Not being a creeper."

She started to laugh. "Thanks. Sorry I fell asleep. I know you're not a creeper. However it does sound like your brother might have known a few guys like that."

"It does. He had some wild days in the NFL," Derek said, going to sit down on the other side of the bed and take off his shoes. He heard her moving behind him as he finished getting undressed. He realized this was what he'd been hoping to find with Bianca. There was an intimacy that living together had brought to his life that he'd never had before. Something that he had always wanted but never thought he'd find.

Thirteen

Bianca watched him moving around getting undressed. He took his watch off first and then pulled his shirt from his trousers and toed off his shoes. This was the casual intimacy that she'd been looking forward to in her marriage but that she'd never had. Sex with Jose had always been on his terms and quick. He'd left her when it was over. The one time with Derek—and sleeping in his arms afterward—was the closest she'd come to spending the night with her lover.

Tonight she wanted more. She was tired of waiting and avoiding him. In their conversation earlier,

Derek had seemed to suggest that he wanted more from her than just something temporary. She was buzzing from the champagne and the festivities. Tonight had changed everything.

She hadn't felt this hopeful about a relationship since she'd found out she was pregnant and thought that would fix her failing marriage. But this change was inspired by Derek.

He'd missed her.

He'd held her close when they danced, lighting a fire deep inside of her. One that would never be put out.

She stood up to get changed but decided that it had been too long since she'd had Derek. She knew it had been her own fault. But now that they were in this room together again, she wanted him.

And there was no reason she couldn't have him.

She striped down to her underwear. She'd worn a pushup strapless bra under the jumpsuit and left it on now. The tops of her breasts spilled out of the fabric. She wore a matching thong.

She turned to check her lipstick in the mirror, planning to touch up the bright berry color she'd used earlier, but when she looked in the mirror her gaze met Derek's. He watched her. His chest was bare and one hand rubbed down over his stomach. He'd taken his pants off and his erection poked through the opening in his boxers.

She canted her hips back and looked over her shoulder at him.

"See something you like?" she asked.

As opposed to the first time they'd been together, tonight she was herself again. The new Bianca, who had the confidence to know that this man wanted her and she could give him something no other woman could.

He sorted of grunted at her and a smile played around her lips.

She pouted as she turned and walked toward him using all the knowledge she'd gained on the catwalk in Paris. She knew how to move her body to draw attention to it.

"Do you think my lips need touching up?" she asked as she rounded the bed where he stood.

"Hell, no. I'm going to kiss the remaining lipstick off your mouth anyway," he said.

"Are you?" she asked. "I thought I was going to leave it on your skin. I was thinking I'd start here. With a kiss on the side of your neck. And then maybe work my way lower."

She touched him with her fingertip on the spot where his pulse beat rapidly and then walked her fingers downward. She skimmed over his nipple and watched him flinch as she continued moving lower. She stopped when she reached his belly button and swirled her finger around it, dipping her finger inside, and then bent forward to swirl her tongue around it. She felt his erection jump and lengthen against her breasts, which she'd deliberately leaned forward to rub against him.

She stood back up and put her hand on his shoulder, going up on tiptoe to bite the lobe of his ear. "Do you think you'd like that?"

He growled a response that sounded like yes and his hands came to her waist and then moved lower to her buttocks, grasping both of her cheeks and lifting her off her feet.

"Part your legs," he said in that low gravelly tone. "Put them around my waist."

"No."

She slithered down his body and away from him. "You sit down. Wait."

He growled deep in her throat when she leaned forward to brush kisses against his chest. Her lips were sweet and not shy as she explored his torso. Then he felt the edge of her teeth as she nibbled at his pecs.

He watched her, his eyes narrowing. Her tongue darted out and brushed against his nipple. She kept doing that to him and he began to realize where she was going with this. He arched off the bed and put his hand on the back of her head, urging her to stay where she was.

She put her hands on his shoulders and eased her

way down his chest tracing each of the muscles that ribbed his abdomen and then slowly making her way lower. He could feel his heartbeat in his erection and he knew he was going to lose it if he didn't take control.

But another part of him wanted to just sit back and let her have her way with him. When she reached the edge of his boxers, she stopped and glanced up at him.

He held himself still, waiting to see what she was going to do next. She grabbed his boxers and carefully pushed them over his hard-on, easing them down his thighs and then leaving him to step out of them.

Her hands were on his erection and then he felt the brush of her lips against his shaft. She stroked him with her fingers and took the tip of him in her mouth. His hands fell to her head as she sucked him into her mouth and his hips canted forward. It had been too long since he'd been with her and he was on the knife's edge of his control.

He pulled her up and she let him. Sitting down on the edge of the bed, he drew her to him. He reached around behind her to undo her bra and when it fell off, he sat back to look at her. She took a half step back and put her hand on her hip, arching her eyebrows at him.

"Like what you see?" she asked.

"Stop teasing me, Bia," he said. "It's been too long and I'm about to lose it."

"Good. You're too controlled. I think you're trying to manage everything about this like you would in the operating room. But this isn't supposed to follow a script. This is supposed to be raw and honest."

"I feel raw," he said.

He pulled down her thong and she stepped out of it. He fingered the soft hair that covered her secrets and then drew her down on his lap, lifting her slightly so that her nipples grazed his chest.

"Now it's my turn," he said.

She nibbled on her lips as he rotated his shoulders so that his chest rubbed against her breasts. She put her hands on his shoulders and arched her back, her center rubbing over his erection.

"This is what I want," she said.

Blood roared in his ears; after months of waiting he wasn't sure of his control. He'd dreamed about this moment every night in the bed where he'd taken her, made her his. She was his fiancée as far as the world was concerned and now he wanted to leave his mark on her.

He was so hard, so full right now, that he needed to be inside of her body. He fumbled for the nightstand and the condoms he'd optimistically put in there earlier in the day. He couldn't get hold of the box but felt her reach around him and grab it.

"Is this what you're looking for?" she asked, holding a foil packet up.

"Yes," he growled.

"Let me," she said, scooting back on his thighs and ripping it open. She put the condom on the tip of his penis and slowly rolled it all the way down. She let her fingers linger lower, caressing him before she looked back at him.

There was a fire in his soul that was being fanned by Bianca. She was everything he'd always wanted but never thought he could have. He pulled her closer, his mouth slamming down on hers. All subtlety was gone. He plunged his tongue into her mouth and tangled his hands in her hair. The pins that held it up fell to the floor. He put one arm around her waist, lifted her up until he could shift his hips and found the opening of her body.

He drove up into her as she bit his tongue. When he was buried inside of her he stopped. He opened his eyes because he wanted to make sure this wasn't another erotic dream that he would wake from feeling frustrated and alone.

Bianca's eyes were open as well and there was fire in her big brown gaze. She shifted up and then slowly lowered herself back down on him. She put her hands on his shoulders as she started to ride him.

He pulled her head down to his so he could taste her mouth. Her mouth opened over his and he told himself to take it slow but slow wasn't in his programming with this woman. She was pure feminine temptation and he had her in his arms. All of the control he'd honed over the years was gone.

He nibbled on her lips and held her at his mercy. Her nails dug into his shoulders and she leaned up, brushing against his chest. Her nipples were hard points and he pulled away from her mouth, glancing down to see them pushing against his chest. Then she arched her back and he felt the brush of her nipple against his lips.

He caressed her back and spine, scraping his nails down the length of it. He followed the line of her back down the indentation above her backside, all the while taking control of the motion of her hips and driving her faster against him.

She closed her eyes and held her breath as he fondled her, running his finger over her nipple. It was velvety compared to the satin smoothness of her breast. He brushed his finger back and forth until she bit her lower lip and shifted on his lap.

He suckled her, used his teeth to tease her and then played with her other nipple with his fingers. She continued to ride him, her pace increasing but it wasn't enough for him. He wanted her.

He needed more.

He scraped his fingernail over her nipple and she shivered in his arms. He pushed her back a little bit so he could see her. Her breasts were bare, nipples distended and begging for his mouth. He lowered his head and suckled.

"You have very pretty breasts, Bianca," he said against her skin. She smelled good here as well, as if she'd spritzed her perfume in her cleavage earlier in the evening.

"Thank you," she said. "I always thought they were on the small side. That's why I wear push-up bras all the time."

He cupped them and looked up at her, their eyes meeting. "They are just right."

She leaned down and kissed him softly and gently. "I'm glad you think so."

He put one hand on the small of her back. With his other hand he pulled the remaining pins from her hair until it fell around her shoulders. He pulled it forward over the front of her chest. She sat straight with her shoulders back, which thrust her breasts up at him. He had a lap full of woman and he knew that he wanted Bianca more than…anything. She wasn't something he could win by working hard and studying, which had always been his way. And leaving her alone hadn't worked, either. It was only now that he had her back in his arms that he realized he was never going to let her go again.

She put her hands on his shoulders and he felt her tighten herself around his shaft as she shifted up on him and started to move again. Her eyes closed and her head fell back. He watched her for a moment until he felt like he was going to explode. But he needed to bring her along with him.

It had been too long and even though he wanted to make this last he knew that he was going to be hard-pressed to do that.

He leaned down and licked her nipple and then blew on it and saw the goose bumps spread down her body. He loved the way she reacted to his mouth on her breasts. He kept his attention on them. She started to ride him harder and faster as he continued touching her there.

He leaned down and licked the valley between her breasts, whispering hot words of carnal need. She responded by digging her nails into his shoulders.

He bit carefully at the white skin of her chest, suckling at her so that he'd leave his mark. He wanted her to remember this moment and what they had done when she was alone later.

He kept kissing her and she rocked her hips harder against his length. He grabbed her hips and held her to him as he slammed up into her. Then he bit down carefully on her tender, aroused nipple. She screamed his name as her body tightened around his and he lifted his mouth to hers to capture her cries of passion.

She continued rocking against him and he slowly

built her passion back to the boiling point again. He suckled her nipple as he rotated his hips to catch her pleasure point with each thrust, and he felt her hands in his hair clenching as she threw her head back the exact moment her climax ripped through her.

He varied his thrusts, finding a rhythm that would draw out the tension at the base of his spine. But she was having none of that and leaned down to whisper in his ear. Telling him how good he felt. And how deeply he filled her. Her words were like a velvet whip on him and he felt his orgasm coming a second before he erupted.

He didn't want this to end. The thought flashed through his mind that the last time after they'd made love things had gone wrong.

"Bianca."

He called her name as he came. She arched over him again and then they collapsed back on the bed in a heap. He held her close and pretended it was just after-sex euphoria but he knew that she was in his heart now.

There was no leaving her. There was no turning back from this. And though he wasn't as sure of what the future would hold he knew that when the board made their decision about who would be chief of cardiology, he wasn't going to come home and break his engagement to Bianca. He wanted her to be his fiancée for real.

Which meant he was going to have to ask her to marry him.

And that was scary. Because she'd agreed to one thing—a temporary engagement. And the last time when he'd asked her for that, the answer hadn't been as important as it would be this time.

He carried her into the adjoining bathroom and they took a shower together. Neither of them talking.

When they climbed back into bed, he held her to him, cuddling her close and knowing that everything had changed. When they'd made love the first time it had fixed something broken in Bianca. This time it had fixed the pieces of him that had always been out of joint, leading him to an important realization.

That he'd finally found the right place for himself, right here in her arms.

Fourteen

The wedding weekend changed a lot between them but when they got back to their routines it was hard not fall back into old habits. But surprisingly, they didn't. The first morning they were back in the house Bianca went downstairs early to see Derek before he left for work. He and Beni were morning people, and she found them chattering away the entire time. They had started a new routine.

Derek changed a few of his other habits, too. Instead of staying home in the evenings when they went up to the club to play tennis he started joining them. As the weeks went by and the board meeting to name the new cardiology chief drew closer she started to feel like they were becoming a family.

So the day of the big announcement was a big deal in her mind. She and Beni planned a special dinner for the three of them and she was pretty proud of the way that Beni had helped her decorate the courtyard.

Cobie was even helping them by hanging some lights she'd found online that were decorated with the caduceus, the symbol for medicine and surgery. She looked around the courtyard and knew that many of the most important moments in her life with Derek had happened here.

"Thanks for helping us get everything set up today," Bianca said to Cobie.

"No problem," he replied. "The little dude promised to help me with my Spanish so we're square."

"*Si*, Mama," Beni said. "Cobie is *muy bueno*."

She smiled as the two of them started speaking in Spanish and realized how Beni had really started to bloom here in Cole's Hill and in Derek's house. He liked having all of his stuff out of storage. She and Derek had taken him shopping in the outlets at San Marcos a few weeks ago to bulk up his room. This place was starting to feel like home.

And that felt right to her since Derek was definitely the man she'd fallen in love with. There was a niggling doubt in the back of her mind that wouldn't be eased until she asked him tonight to marry her. It was funny how everything here had started out temporary in theory but from the moment she'd started talking to Derek and they'd moved together, everything had been more real than it ever had been with Jose.

Being with Derek had shown her that what she'd felt for Jose had been infatuation and a little bit of oh-my-God-I-can't-believe-this-is-my-life. There was none of that with Derek. There was just living in the town she loved and building a family with him and Beni.

She had something she'd never expected to find with anyone after Jose left. A part of her had been afraid that another man wouldn't be able to love her son the way she did. But Derek was really good with Benito. Even when the two of them had been keeping their distance, he'd still made time for her son. It had shown her that Derek Caruthers was a man of his word. And when he made a promise he kept it.

The doorbell rang, and since Cobie was helping Beni to wrap some lights around one of the trees, she waved for him to stay and went to answer it.

She opened the door to see Kinley and Penny standing there. Penny had on a cowboy hat, a pair of jeans and a T-shirt with a ballerina on it.

"Howdy," Penny said.

"Howdy," Bianca responded, stepping back and gesturing for them to come in.

"I got the cake you asked for from the bakery," Kinley said, handing the box over to her.

"Thank you. I wasn't sure I'd have time to get it before Derek comes home."

"Any word from him yet?"

"Nothing. I can only assume he's still in the meeting," Bianca said.

Kinley's phone pinged and she looked down at it. "That man. I told Nate we should turn on Find My Friends on our phones since he drives fast and I was worried about him having an accident on his way from town to the ranch."

"Okay. So what does that have to do with anything?" Bianca asked.

"He can see I'm at your place and wants to know if you've heard from Derek," Kinley said.

Bianca had to smile. One of the things she loved about the Caruthers family was the closeness between the brothers. She was glad that Beni would have more uncles.

"No, nosey, she hasn't," Kinley said out loud as she typed. "Okay, do you need me to help with anything?"

"Not really. I think everything is almost ready. Just waiting for Derek," Bianca said.

She patted the pocket of her pants where she'd slipped the ring box earlier. She had every last detail planned and now all she could do was wait. She decided to text Derek to see if he'd heard any news.

Any word yet?

Yes. Good news. I am the new Chief of Cardiology. Bad news three-car accident on the highway. Going into surgery now.

Congratulations. See you tonight.

Can't wait. <3

"Derek got the chief position," Bianca told Kinley.

"That's great," Kinley said. "Was there a chance he wouldn't get it?"

"Yes. I mean, he's brilliant and everything but he's still sort of young for the position. Plus, Dr. Masters joined the board to oversee the cardiac surgical wing and name the new head, and she and Derek had some past…relations."

"Relations?" Kinley asked with a laugh.

"I know that sounds dumb, right? They dated. And when they broke up she wasn't ready to move on. So she was sort of not happy with him on a personal level. I'm glad she's finally past that."

"Me too."

Kinley and Penny visited for a few hours, but by

then, Bianca's elation had turned to worry. There was still no text from Derek that he was out of surgery. Her guests went home, Cobie retreated to the pool house and it was just her and Benito in the house. She tried to distract herself by watching him race his car around the backyard on the cone track that Derek had laid out for him. But when the time for dinner came around and there was still no word from Derek she was starting to despair.

She finally texted him to check if he was out of the operating theater. She got no response. And though she didn't want to be the type of woman who had to call around to find her man—she'd done that with Jose—she finally called the hospital and learned he was in surgery. The receptionist then forwarded her call to the cardiac wing so she could get an update from the assistant.

The fear and doubt that had been building inside of her dissipated as she heard the nurse's reassuring voice. It was hard to think that she was still dealing with trust issues. Derek wasn't interested in another woman. He had dedicated the last two months to her. Even the month when they'd been sort of avoiding each other.

"Could you let me know when Dr. Caruthers is out of surgery?" Bianca asked the nurse after they'd exchanged greetings. The nurse was pleasant and chatty, and Bianca decided she'd been worrying for nothing.

Until what the woman said next stopped her dead in her tracks.

"Ma'am, he left the hospital at least an hour ago."

Derek was exhausted as he and Raine left the operating room and went into the post-op area to clean up. They still had to see the family and talk to the other surgeon who would do the follow-up surgery for the other injuries sustained by his patient. The car accident had been pretty horrible and the medevac had brought three patients to their hospital and airlifted two others to Houston.

It had been a long day and he was looking forward to getting home to Bianca and Beni and having a low-key evening. He'd operated on the six-year-old girl who had been seated behind the driver. The driver was still in surgery. The point of impact had been on the driver's side and those passengers had sustained the most threatening injuries. The mother and two siblings had various fractures and lacerations but weren't being admitted to the hospital. When Derek walked into that waiting room and saw them sitting there, he had a flash of how he'd feel if it were Bianca and Beni in the operating room.

He sat down and updated them on the status of their daughter and then let Raine take over so he could go home to Bianca. But then he had to answer a text from his brothers and he noticed one from Bianca as well. He told her he'd be leaving soon. He needed to see her and make sure she was okay. He didn't bother with a shower and just went to the parking lot. But he stopped when he saw Marnie leaning against his car.

"I take it your patient is doing well?" she asked as he approached.

"Yes. She'll make a full recovery."

"Good to hear. You really are a miracle worker when you're in the operating room," she said. "Sorry I made you jump through hoops before naming you chief."

"It's okay," he said. Actually, without Marnie's delaying tactics he would have continued on his path, never realizing what he was missing. He'd never have asked Bianca to be his fake fiancée. In a way, he thought he should be thanking Marnie.

"You made me realize how single-focus my life had become. I'm glad you forced my hand," he said.

She nodded and then gave him a hard look. "I hate it that you are marrying someone else."

"That's just because you don't like to lose," he said. "You don't love me."

She tipped her head to the side and studied him for a very long time. "You're right. I don't love you. You're too independent. I guess I tried to make it so you would need me but the more I tried that the farther away you got."

"We just weren't meant for each other," he said. "You'll find someone who will be right for you just like I have Bianca."

She nodded. "I hope so."

"I know so. The right man is going to fall at your feet, Marnie."

She gave him a quick smile. "From your lips to God's ears. 'Night, Derek."

"Good night, Marnie," he said, unlocking his door and getting into the car. As soon as he was behind the wheel, he took a deep breath. He wasn't ready to drive. He sat there, thinking. In the old days he would have gone to see Nate. That little girl had reminded him of Benito and he had never been so scared in the operating room. Once he started focusing on the heart and the operation his mind had cleared but when he'd first looked down at that little body, he'd realized how much his life had changed.

He had a family of his own now and keeping them safe was the only thing that really mattered to him. He took his phone out to text Bianca and let her know he was on his way home and saw he'd missed a text from her.

Where are you? The hospital said you left an hour ago.

He quickly typed his reply.

Sorry, got caught up talking to the family and then Marnie. On my way home now.

There was no further response and he scrubbed his hand over his face. He put the car in gear and drove home as fast—and safely—as he could. Within twenty minutes, he'd pulled into the driveway of his house and then let himself in.

Benito came running up to him and he bent down and scooped the little boy up. He was so happy to see him healthy. He glanced over Beni's head at Bianca and saw that she had her arms wrapped around her waist.

He knew she was upset about something but he only knew that his heart was so full of love for her that he needed to hold her and tell her.

He carried Benito in his arms over to her and hugged her close. She was stiff for a moment and then she relented and put her arms around them. He held these two people who had come to mean more to him than life itself in his arms for a few minutes until Beni squirmed to get down and excitedly told them to follow him to the courtyard.

The first thing Derek saw were the lights and the table. He stopped next to it and realized how very lucky he was to have decided to ask Bianca to be his fake fiancée. The only thing left to do was to make this real. She was already in his heart and in his mind he was planning a wedding for them soon.

Bianca saw the fatigue on Derek's face and she wanted to give him the benefit of the doubt. But he'd told her he had been talking with Marnie instead of just coming home to her. She wasn't sure how much of her jealousy and unease was from Derek and how much of it was left over from Jose.

Plus, what if he'd had to do something else in order to convince Marnie to give him the job? But she knew Derek. Or at least she thought she had. He wasn't the kind of man who would betray her like that. Was he?

She and Benito led Derek out onto the courtyard patio where they'd set up dinner. The lights were on and the medical paraphernalia that she'd gotten to decorate the table were all in perfect position. She'd blogged about making every little thing in life special and her readers had given her some good feedback but now she was afraid she was a fraud. She was falling apart because her fiancé hadn't texted her right back.

"Wait!" Benito exclaimed. He ran back into the house and Derek looked over at her.

"What's he up to?" Derek asked.

"He has a surprise for you," Bianca said. Beni had wanted to dress like a doctor, like Derek.

"Poppi, look at me," the little boy said when he came back out on the patio. He had on a pair of scrubs and a stethoscope around his neck.

Bianca glanced at Derek and saw that moment of vulnerability and love on his face as her son called him Poppi.

"I'm like you," Beni said.

"I couldn't be prouder," Derek said. He scooped Beni up. The two of them chatted during dinner and Bianca sat there trying to reconcile the two images she had of Derek in her mind: the man who'd spent an hour with his former girlfriend and the guy who was learning Spanish and talking to her son about any topic the toddler wanted to discuss.

That love she felt for Derek grew stronger but her doubts held it trapped. She was afraid to let herself believe in him…believe in them. She watched him for a sign. Something that would show her that he was ready for the change that she wanted them to make as a couple.

At the end of the meal she was still waiting for a sign of what she should do next. She decided to keep the ring in her pocket. Asking a man to marry her seemed like a big risk when she wasn't sure if she'd fooled herself into believing in something that might not be real.

After Beni was bathed and put in bed she went back downstairs to find Derek. He was in the den talking on the phone and she hesitated in the doorway unsure if she should go in or not.

But he waved her inside and she came in and sat on one of the padded leather armchairs while he finished up his call.

"Sorry, that was Nate. He wanted to talk and this is the first chance I had," Derek said. "Did you get Benito put to bed?"

"Yes," she said. "He was very excited for you even though he has no idea what your promotion means."

"He's a sweet boy," Derek said, coming around to sit in the chair next to her. "I am starting to think of him as my son."

Those were words that would have warmed her heart earlier in the day, but now with doubts and old fears dominating her thoughts, it was hard.

"That's nice."

Derek leaned away from her and looked at her out from under that mop of bangs that had fallen forward. She didn't want to be charmed by how he looked but she always was. She always saw the boy who'd been her friend long before they'd been attracted to each other, when his hair was rumpled like it was now. She wanted to trust Derek.

She wanted to believe that he was just talking with his ex-girlfriend for some innocent reason instead of returning Bianca's texts and getting home to her. And a part of her knew all she had to do was ask him. Derek wasn't Jose, who would tell her sweet lies that she'd know better than to believe. Derek was blunt and honest.

"What's up? You haven't been yourself since I got home," he said. "Did something happen today? I'm sorry I've been so focused on my day I didn't even think to ask you."

She had that first inkling that her trust in him wasn't misplaced. "My day was fine. No bad news."

"What is it then?" he asked.

She took a deep breath and knew she had to just say it out loud. Now that she was sitting here next to him she felt almost silly about her suspicions but she couldn't just dismiss them.

"Why were you talking with Marnie?" she asked. "I was worried about you and called the hospital and they said you'd left an hour before you texted me."

Derek rubbed his hand over his face and she studied him. She was looking to see if he'd avoid making eye contact with her or get angry that she'd asked him.

"Sorry. She cornered me at my car. We talked. I realized that if it weren't for her and the pressure I'd felt I would never have asked you to be my fake fiancée. I wouldn't have even asked you out on a date, Bia."

She knew that. They had been friends but she saw now that they both had been careful to keep parts of their lives hidden. It had worked for them for a long time. "I know. Why was that?"

"I think I was afraid to see you as anything more than a friend," he said.

"Me, too," she admitted. "Being friends was so much easier than this. I was nice and safely living my life and pretending that you were still the boy who'd been my friend in middle school. But to be honest I'd noticed you'd changed."

"Same. So what's changed tonight?"

She took a deep breath. "I was jealous when I realized that you were with her."

Fifteen

Jealous.

He looked over at her sitting there in her short-sleeved blouse with the wide-legged trousers and realized how sophisticated she looked. He felt like a country bumpkin next to her.

And she was jealous.

She never had to be. He knew that but Bianca didn't. Could he convince her of that truth?

"Of Marnie? She's completely out of the picture," Derek said.

"I know that here," she said pointing to her head. "But my heart isn't so sure."

He leaned forward, putting his arms on his legs and his head in his hands. "I'm not that kind of guy, Bianca. I mean, I might have never been able to commit to a woman for the long term but I've never been the kind of guy who needed to date more than one woman at a time to prove something to myself."

He suspected her fears were based in her previous marriage and if he were being totally honest with himself he knew he'd contributed a little bit by the way he'd asked her to be his pretend fiancée instead of his real one. At the time he hadn't been capable of doing it any other way but now he knew it had been a mistake. He loved her.

He would do whatever he had to in order to make sure she understood.

"I know that. I mean, there's a part of me that can't believe that I even had to bring it up, but I do. I know it's not fair of me to ask you to pay for someone else's damage—"

"You're not asking," he said. "It's not a problem. I am the one who came over to you at the club that night. I'm the one who changed our dynamic. And I know that I've fallen in love with you."

He shifted around in his chair to face her and then reached over to take her hands. He wanted to make her understand that he was willing to give her as much time as she needed to feel safe with him. To believe in him and the love he had for her. She'd been conned by a world-class Casanova and he didn't want to do anything that would hurt her.

"You love me?"

"Yes. I didn't mean to blurt it out like that but I've known it since you moved in. I missed you every time you were gone, and Beni too. I started to realize what it meant to have a family of my own. But I also know that I asked you to do me a favor and now I'm changing that by telling you how I feel. I don't want you to feel trapped."

"I'm not trapped. I'm sorry about the jealousy. It took me by surprise because a part of me knows that you are nothing like Jose. But then I remembered the big show that our engagement was and how you and I started out as just..."

"Pretend. I think I was lying to myself even then," he said. With Bianca he didn't want to play games. When he'd seen that little girl on the operating table tonight he'd realized how fragile life was. He didn't want to waste another minute of his time with her.

He needed her to know how much she meant to him.

"This isn't going to change," he said, taking her hand and putting it over his heart. "My love for you has been a part of me for a long time. And at first it was the love of friends but it has grown and I want you to be my partner in life. I want to be Beni's father and I want us to give him brothers and sisters. I want everything when I look into your eyes, Bianca."

He felt her hand under his start to shake a little and she gave him the sweetest smile he'd ever seen on her face before pulling her hand free of his.

She stood up, and then went down on one knee in front of him.

"What are you doing?"

"I love you, Derek Caruthers. I never thought I would say this to another man but the last two months have showed me that the dreams I'd had of what life could be were possible with the right person."

"Get up," Derek said. "You've shown the same thing to me."

She shook her head and he shifted until he was kneeling next to her on the carpeted floor.

"What are you doing?" he asked her.

"Something that I should have done a while ago but I wanted to wait until we gave our temporary arrangement a real shot."

"Okay," he said, though he wasn't sure what she was getting at.

Then she reached into her pocket and took out a ring box. He felt his heart melt. The love he felt for her swelled and he couldn't quite believe what he was seeing.

"Derek Caruthers, will you marry me? Will you

be my husband and partner and father to my children? Will you love me forever?"

"I will," he said. He leaned in and kissed her. He wanted to keep the embrace light but this was Bianca and they'd just decided to make their engagement real. When he lifted his head they were both breathing heavy. He stood up, drew her to feet and carried her into his bedroom.

He set her on the middle of his bed and remembered the first time they'd made love. That was the moment when he'd realized how much Bianca meant to him and that he was probably never going to be able to let her go.

"Wait a minute. You haven't put your ring on yet."

He opened the box and saw that it was a man's signet ring with a caduceus in the middle and a raised stone with their initials linked together in it.

He put it on his finger and then made love to Bianca. He had thought that his career was the one thing that would define him. But he found that living with Bianca and Beni had shown him who he really was. He was a surgeon yes and a brother and a son, but he was also a father, a friend and a lover. And it was more than he'd thought he'd ever call his own.

* * * * *

Don't miss any of these novels from
USA TODAY *bestselling author*
Katherine Garbera!

THE TYCOON'S BABY SURPRISE
HIS BABY AGENDA
HIS SEDUCTION GAME PLAN
HIS INSTANT HEIR
BOUND BY A CHILD

Available now from Harlequin Desire!

***

If you're on Twitter, tell us what you think of Harlequin Desire! #harlequindesire.

COMING NEXT MONTH FROM

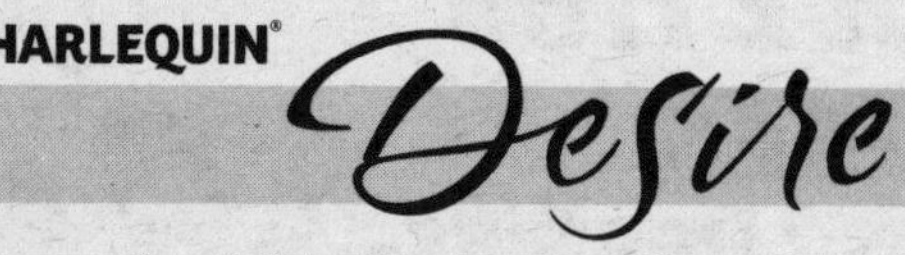

Available August 8, 2017

#2533 THE CEO'S NANNY AFFAIR

Billionaires and Babies • by Joss Wood

When billionaire Linc Ballantyne's ex abandons not one, but *two* children, he strikes up a wary deal with her too-sexy sister. She'll be the nanny and they'll keep their hands to themselves. But their temporary truce soon becomes a temporary tryst!

#2534 TEMPTED BY THE WRONG TWIN

Texas Cattleman's Club: Blackmail • by Rachel Bailey

Harper Lake is pregnant, but the father isn't who she thinks—it's her boss's identical twin brother! Wealthy former Navy SEAL Nick Tate pretended to be his brother as a favor, and now he's proposing a marriage of convenience that just might lead to real romance...

#2535 THE TEXAN'S BABY PROPOSAL

Callahan's Clan • by Sara Orwig

Millionaire Texan Marc Medina must marry immediately to inherit his grandfather's ranch. When his newly single secretary tells him she's pregnant, he knows a brilliant deal when he sees one. He'll make her his wife...and have her in his bed!

#2536 LITTLE SECRETS: CLAIMING HIS PREGNANT BRIDE by Sarah M. Anderson

Restless—that's businessman and biker Seth Bolton. But when he rescues pregnant runaway bride Kate Burroughs, he wants much more than he should with the lush mom-to-be... But she won't settle for anything less than taming his heart!

#2537 FROM TEMPTATION TO TWINS

Whiskey Bay Brides • by Barbara Dunlop

When Juliet Parker goes home to reopen her grandfather's restaurant, she clashes with her childhood crush, tycoon Caleb Watford, who's building a rival restaurant. Then the stakes skyrocket after their one night leaves her expecting two little surprises!

#2538 THE TYCOON'S FIANCÉE DEAL

The Wild Caruthers Bachelors • by Katherine Garbera

Derek Caruthers promised his best friend that their fake engagement would end after he'd secured his promotion...but what's a man of honor to do when their red-hot kisses prove she's the only one for him?

YOU CAN FIND MORE INFORMATION ON UPCOMING HARLEQUIN® TITLES, FREE EXCERPTS AND MORE AT WWW.HARLEQUIN.COM.

HDCNM0717

Get 2 Free Books, Plus 2 Free Gifts— just for trying the Reader Service!

HARLEQUIN Desire

YES! Please send me 2 FREE Harlequin® Desire novels and my 2 FREE gifts (gifts are worth about $10 retail). After receiving them, if I don't wish to receive any more books, I can return the shipping statement marked "cancel." If I don't cancel, I will receive 6 brand-new novels every month and be billed just $4.55 per book in the U.S. or $5.24 per book in Canada. That's a savings of at least 13% off the cover price! It's quite a bargain! Shipping and handling is just 50¢ per book in the U.S. and 75¢ per book in Canada.* I understand that accepting the 2 free books and gifts places me under no obligation to buy anything. I can always return a shipment and cancel at any time. The free books and gifts are mine to keep no matter what I decide.

225/326 HDN GMRV

Name (PLEASE PRINT)

Address Apt. #

City State/Prov. Zip/Postal Code

Signature (if under 18, a parent or guardian must sign)

Mail to the **Reader Service:**
IN U.S.A.: P.O. Box 1341, Buffalo, NY 14240-8531
IN CANADA: P.O. Box 603, Fort Erie, Ontario L2A 5X3

Want to try two free books from another line?
Call 1-800-873-8635 or visit www.ReaderService.com.

*Terms and prices subject to change without notice. Prices do not include applicable taxes. Sales tax applicable in N.Y. Canadian residents will be charged applicable taxes. Offer not valid in Quebec. This offer is limited to one order per household. Books received may not be as shown. Not valid for current subscribers to Harlequin Desire books. All orders subject to approval. Credit or debit balances in a customer's account(s) may be offset by any other outstanding balance owed by or to the customer. Please allow 4 to 6 weeks for delivery. Offer available while quantities last.

Your Privacy—The Reader Service is committed to protecting your privacy. Our Privacy Policy is available online at www.ReaderService.com or upon request from the Reader Service.

We make a portion of our mailing list available to reputable third parties that offer products we believe may interest you. If you prefer that we not exchange your name with third parties, or if you wish to clarify or modify your communication preferences, please visit us at www.ReaderService.com/consumerschoice or write to us at Reader Service Preference Service, P.O. Box 9062, Buffalo, NY 14240-9062. Include your complete name and address.

HD17R2

SPECIAL EXCERPT FROM

Ready or not, love will find a way,
even when confronted with the most reluctant of hearts...

Read on for a sneak peek of the next
***GUTHRIE BROTHERS** book, WORTH THE WAIT,*
from New York Times *bestselling author Lori Foster!*

Violet, looking messier than Hogan had ever seen her, was leaning over the papers again scattered across her desk.

"Violet?"

Slowly she turned her face toward him.

Her bloodshot eyes surprised him. Sick. He stepped in farther. "Hey, you okay?"

She looked from him to the paperwork. "I don't know." More coughs racked her.

Hogan strode forward and put a hand to her forehead. "Shit. You're burning up."

"What time is it?"

"A few minutes after midnight."

"Oh." She pushed back from the desk but didn't make it far. "The restaurant," she gasped in between strained breaths.

"I took care of it." Holding her elbow, he helped to support her as she stood. His most pressing thought was getting her home and in bed. No, not the way he'd like, but definitely the way she needed. "Where are your car keys?"

Unsteady on her feet, she frowned. "What do you mean, you took care of it?"

"You have good employees—you know that. They're aware of the routine. Colt pitched in, too. Everything is done."

"But…"

"I double-checked. I'm not incompetent, so trust me."

Her frown darkened.

"You can thank me, Violet."

She tried to look stern, coughed again and gave up. "Thank you." Still she kept one hand on the desk. "I'm just so blasted tired."

"I know." He eased her into his side, his arm around her. "Come on. Let me drive you home." Then he found her purse and without a qualm, dug through it for her keys.

He found them. He also found two condoms. His gaze flashed to hers, but her eyes were closed and she looked asleep on her feet, her body utterly boneless as she drew in shallow, strained breaths.

"Come on." With an arm around her, her purse and keys held in his free hand, he led her out the back way to the employee lot, securing the door behind her. Her yellow Mustang shone bright beneath security lights.

His bike would be okay. Or at least, it better be.

Violet tried to get herself together but it wasn't easy. She honestly felt like she could close her eyes and nod right off. "The trash—"

"Was taken out." He opened the passenger door and helped her in.

"If you left on even one fan—"

"It would set off the security sensors. I know. They're all off." He fastened her seat belt around her and closed her door.

As soon as he slid behind the wheel, she said, "But the end-of-day reports—"

"Are done." He started her car. "Try not to worry, okay?"

Easier said than done.

Because the town was so small, Hogan seemed to know where she lived even though she'd never had him over. She hadn't dared.

Hogan in her home? Nope. Not a good idea.

Even feeling miserable, her head pounding and her chest aching, she was acutely aware of him beside her in the enclosed car, and the way he kept glancing at her. He tempted her, always had, from the first day she'd met him.

He was also a major runaround. Supposedly a reformed runaround, but she didn't trust in that. Things had happened with his late wife, things that had made him bitter and unpredictable.

Yet no less appealing.

She wasn't one to pry; otherwise she might have gotten all the details from Honor, his sister-in-law, already. She figured if he ever wanted to, Hogan himself would tell her. Not that there was any reason, since she would not get involved with him.

Hogan was fun to tease, like watching the flames in a bonfire. You watched, you enjoyed, but you did not jump in the fire. She needed Hogan Guthrie, but she wasn't a stupid woman, so she tried to never court trouble.

Don't miss WORTH THE WAIT
by New York Times *bestselling author Lori Foster!*

Copyright © 2017 by Lori Foster

PHEXPLF967

EXCLUSIVE LIMITED TIME OFFER AT

www.HARLEQUIN.com

$15.99 U.S./$19.99 CAN.

$1.50 OFF

New York Times Bestselling Author

LORI FOSTER

worth the wait

Ready or not...
love will find a way

Available July 25, 2017.
Get your copy today!

Receive $1.50 OFF the purchase price of WORTH THE WAIT by Lori Foster when you use the coupon code below on Harlequin.com.

LFWORTHIT

Offer valid from July 25, 2017, until August 31, 2017, on www.Harlequin.com.

Valid in the U.S.A. and Canada only. To redeem this offer, please add the print or ebook version of WORTH THE WAIT by Lori Foster to your shopping cart and then enter the coupon code at checkout.

DISCLAIMER: Offer valid on the print or ebook version of WORTH THE WAIT by Lori Foster from July 25, 2017, at 12:01 a.m. ET until August 31, 2017, 11:59 p.m. ET at www.Harlequin.com only. The Customer will receive $1.50 OFF the list price of WORTH THE WAIT by Lori Foster in print or ebook on www.Harlequin.com with the **LFWORTHIT** coupon code. Sales tax applied where applicable. Quantities are limited. Valid in the U.S.A. and Canada only. All orders subject to approval.

www.HQNBooks.com

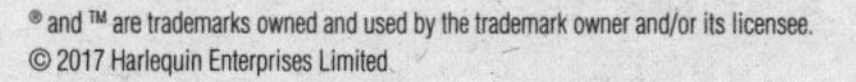
® and ™ are trademarks owned and used by the trademark owner and/or its licensee.
© 2017 Harlequin Enterprises Limited

PHCOUPLFHD0817

LOVE
Harlequin romance?

Join our Harlequin community to share your thoughts and connect with other romance readers!

Be the first to find out about promotions, news, and exclusive content!

Sign up for the Harlequin e-newsletter and download a free book from any series at

www.TryHarlequin.com

CONNECT WITH US AT:

Harlequin.com/Community

Facebook.com/HarlequinBooks

Twitter.com/HarlequinBooks

Instagram.com/HarlequinBooks

Pinterest.com/HarlequinBooks

ReaderService.com

ROMANCE WHEN YOU NEED IT

HSOCIAL2017

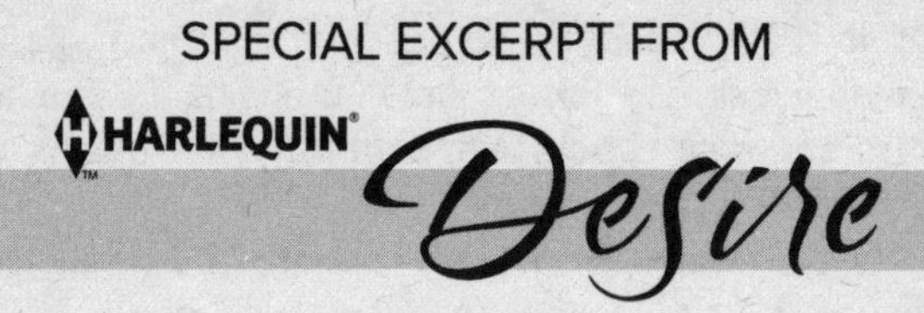

When he proposed to Katrina Morrison, wealthy hotelier Jonas Halstead made it very *clear their marriage would be in name only to save his inheritance. So why is* he *the one falling in love?*

Read on for a sneak peek at CONVENIENT CINDERELLA BRIDE by Joss Wood, part of the sizzling ***SECRETS OF THE A-LIST*** *series.*

Jonas was impeccably dressed.

Kat's eyes traveled over a broad chest and wide shoulders, up a tanned neck to a strong jaw covered with two-day-old stubble. A mouth that was slow to smile but still sexy. Rich, successful and hot.

He had a rep for being a bit of a bastard, in business and in bed. That fact only dropped his sexy factor by a quarter of a percent.

"Mr. Halstead, welcome back to El Acantilado," Kat murmured, ignoring her jumping heart.

"Call me Jonas."

It wasn't the first time he'd made the offer, but Kat had no intention of accepting. It wasn't professional, and formality kept a healthy distance between her and guys in fancy suits. Like her ex-husband, and sadly, just like her father, those kinds of men were not to be trusted.

HDEXP082017

But it really annoyed Kat that a thousand sparks danced on her skin as Jonas's smile turned his face in her mind from remote-but-still-hot to oh-my-God-I want-to-rip-his-clothes-off.

No. Sexy billionaires were *not* her type. She'd married, and divorced, a ruthless and merciless rich guy.

But it sure felt like she had the screaming hots for a man she shouldn't.

And it was all Jonas Halstead's fault.

Don't miss
CONVENIENT CINDERELLA BRIDE
by Joss Wood,
available September 2017 wherever
Harlequin® Desire® books and ebooks are sold.

www.Harlequin.com

Copyright © 2017 by Joss Wood

HDEXP082017